DESTINATION STARDUST

A NOVEL

CINDY HIDAY

The characters and events in this book are fictitious. Any similarity to real persons, living or dead, is coincidental and not intended by the author.

The demolition date of the Stardust Hotel and Casino has been changed for the sake of the story, though the author stayed true to the year and time of day. The Associated Press headline quoted in chapter one was published November 1, 2006. Actual demolition of the Stardust took place early on the morning of March 13, 2007.

For Mom

Other titles by Cindy Hiday

Come Snowfall
Iditarod Nights
Her Phoenix Heart
A Bed of Roses

1: Out Of Time

Ray ran. He didn't know how close the silver car followed behind him. He couldn't hear anything inside his motorcycle helmet but his heart pounding to keep up with his feet. He didn't dare look back and risk slowing or losing his footing.

A stab of pain low in his left side drove him off balance. He lost his grip on the leather bag. Momentum tumbled him into the red Arizona dust – once, twice. He came to a stop flat on his back in a shallow depression perpendicular to the dry wash. The wind knocked out of him and his side on fire, Ray squeezed his eyes shut against the glare of the late afternoon sun. He'd lost his sunglasses somewhere. Sweat leaked from every pore beneath his black leather pants and jacket. His chest rose and fell with each labored breath. The hitch in his side throbbed. He hadn't run like that since high school.

Seconds later the roar of an engine drowned out the drum of his pulse. Ray opened his eyes as the car hit the lip of the depression. He tensed, expecting to be crushed, but the car flew over him and bounced down hard on the other side, its rear wheels spitting a gravel rooster tail as it sped away.

Ray sputtered and shook dirt from his face. He didn't get a look at the driver, but it had to be the same Johnny asshole who had been on their tail since Oklahoma. Either he didn't see the human speed bump he sailed over, or he found the bag and didn't give a damn. If he found the bag, it wouldn't take him long to realize the contents came up short. Real short.

Ray sat up to a fresh stab of pain. He looked down and discovered the hole low on the left side of his leather jacket. Drawing the jacket open, he stared at the blood stain on his white t-shirt.

"Crap, I'm shot again."

He would have found the irony of it amusing, but the wound concerned him a mite. He removed his helmet, shrugged out of his jacket and worked the t-shirt off, pulling the bottom up and sliding his head out first to keep from smearing blood on his face. The motion tugged the gauze and tape on his shoulder – his first gunshot wound. He looked down at the red seeping from his side and felt queasy. Blood did that to him, especially his own. Swallowing hard, he used a clean corner of the t-shirt to dab the wound and inhaled a hiss at the contact. The blood cleared and he saw a jagged graze across his skin, but no hole.

Ray gave a wry croak that scraped the back of his parched throat. What were the odds of getting shot twice in the same week and losing only a few layers of hide each time? Downright miraculous, he thought, if a body chose to believe in miracles. A lot of unbelievable things had happened since he and Benny left Ohio. The past few days had been anything but boring.

~~~

It all started with boredom. That's what Ray told himself. He retired five months ago, on his sixty-second birthday, and became a widow three months later. His life yawned dark and sleepless ahead of him. Slouched in the worn cushions at one end of the sofa, the drapes drawn against the leaden midday August humidity, he watched Thelma and Louise clasp hands and fly off the edge of the Grand Canyon in Louise's green convertible for what felt like the hundredth time. He longed to be in the car with them. He longed to put an end to his insomnia.

His eleven-year-old son, Benny, sat cross-legged on the carpet a few feet from the screen, rapt in the movie as if seeing it for the first time. The boy's short brown hair clung in damp spikes to the back of his broad neck, his rounded shoulders hunched, a line of sweat staining the back of his Terminator t-shirt. It troubled Ray that his son spent so much time watching movies, but it was something Benny and his mama had done together. Ray hesitated to take that connection away so soon after Virginia's death.

And he hesitated to leave Benny alone. He wanted to reassure his son that Dad wouldn't die in his sleep like Mama did, that Dad would always be there, even if it meant sitting through movie after movie. Even if it was a lie. Ray had no reason to believe Benny wouldn't outlive him, in spite of doctors who warned him of the health risks associated with Down syndrome. He knew his daughter, Karen, would take care of her little brother when the time came. She doted on Benny and had been his fiercest defender from day one.

Maybe it's myself I'm protecting. Maybe I don't like being alone with my boredom.

Or I'm afraid to be.

"Dad?"

Pulled from his thoughts, Ray focused on the soft, heavy contours of Benny's face. "What, son?"

"Let's go."

The *s* stopped short of making its way around the boy's tongue. His thick speech had a pronounced lisp, but Ray understood him fine. The words, at least. "Go where?"

Benny gave the montage images of Thelma and Louise with the credits rolling over them a quick glance. The intensity in his crescent-shaped brown eyes tingled up Ray's spine, as though the boy had opened a door and looked inside his head.

"The Goddamngrandcanyon," Benny said, his answer shooting out as one long word.

Like he'd heard Louise say it in the movie again and again. Ray gave a brief smile. "Just the Grand Canyon. No swearing."

Benny's cheeks reddened. "Sorry." He glanced at the TV screen, then back at Ray. "Let's go," he repeated with a huff of impatience, as if needing an answer before the movie credits ended.

Ray hadn't been to the Grand Canyon since the time he borrowed a buddy's Harley and headed east on leave from Edwards Air Force Base forty years ago. He drove through the Mojave Desert and spent a week camping along the south ridge of the canyon. There'd been a time when he and Virginia planned to buy a Harley and tour the states, once Karen was old enough to be on her own. But then Benny came along. With a wife and two kids to support on a maintenance supervisor's salary, family vacations became few and far between.

Benny continued to stare at him, waiting for an answer. Ray thought of the nightmares the boy had been having since his mama's death – two months of ranting and slapping himself awake. He thought of his own insomnia, the fear that clawed up his back when unconsciousness closed in. Maybe getting away for a while, putting some distance on the memories that haunted them here in this house, would do them both good.

Ray asked, "Are you sure?" and realized Louise had asked the same thing of Thelma before she tromped on the gas peddle and hurled them into the great beyond.

The movie ended and Benny hoisted

himself off the floor with a theatrical grunt. Shuffling his squat legs as though he had feet of lead, he plopped onto the couch hard enough to pop Ray up from the cushions.

"Yeah, Dad. Let's go."

~~~

Now Ray oozed blood and sweat somewhere southwest of Flagstaff. He'd left the motorcycle behind him with a flat tire. The Harley Davidson Softail touring bike wasn't designed to be taken off-road, especially with a sidecar. And especially over some of God's roughest terrain. Ridges and spires of red sedimentary rock stacked like crazy layer cakes bordered the dry wash he had steered the bike onto, attempting to put distance on their trigger-happy pursuer. He hoped to figure a way out of this cat and mouse game before anybody's aim got better.

He struggled to his feet, rolled his t-shirt lengthwise and tied it around his waist to put pressure on the wound. Not pretty, but it would do for the time being. Then he shrugged back into his leather jacket and picked up his helmet. A high-pitched *keek-ik-ik-ik* drew his gaze skyward. He saw the white head and tail of a Bald Eagle as its massive wingspan blocked the sun.

The eagle will guide you.

The thought entered Ray's head as clear as if somebody whispered in his ear, and he felt that tingle up his spine. He squinted against the afternoon heat shimmering off the semi-arid landscape. Benny is with the bike, he assured himself. Where you should be.

Looking back along the dry wash, Ray saw a glint of chrome. He drew up straight and pressed his hand to the pain in his side. He found his sunglasses crushed in the middle of a tire track.

~~~

Things happened too fast for Benny to think right. They lost Grace and the Black Pearl had a flat tire and the bad man kept shooting at them. Dad pushed him toward a pile of big rocks and yelled at him to "Hide!" The look in his eyes told Benny not to argue, just do it. He squatted behind the rocks and heard his dad shout, "I'll be back!"

Just like the Terminator.

Benny peeked out from his hiding place and saw his dad run away with the bag, his long legs flying like the wind blows. Benny never saw him run so fast before. He heard the silver car coming and ducked low. He held his breath so the bad man wouldn't hear him. It had to be the man named Johnny. He must have bought a new car after the red one got shot up. Benny worried that Johnny might try to hurt him because of what he did. He heard the car stop and the door open. It sounded like Johnny was messing with the Black Pearl, probably looking for his money. But Benny knew he wouldn't find it.

Johnny said a bad word – said it three times – then got back into his new car and drove away fast, spinning his wheels in the dirt. Small pebbles flew over to Benny's hiding spot and bounced off his helmet. When it got quiet, Benny snuck around the rocks, keeping low in case Johnny tried to trick him.

"Oh, man." Johnny threw their clothes all over the place. One of Grace's pretty blouses was wadded up on the ground, getting dirty. Benny shook it off and put it back in the saddlebag. Everything needed to be folded again. They might have to find another Laundromat.

A sharp sound echoed off the rock walls and made him jump. A gunshot.

Johnny's shooting at Dad! I need to save him!

But Dad told him to stay put. He might get in trouble and make things worse if he didn't do the right thing.

Don't be a stupid boy! Think!

Then he remembered how he could sometimes make his thoughts happen. Sometimes. If he thought hard enough. A long time ago he saw somebody in a movie, a boy younger than him, send messages that way. He couldn't remember the name of the movie, but he understood about sending. He tried it before, with easy things mostly. One time he really, really wanted pizza for dinner and Mama said, "It's too hot to cook. Let's order pizza!" Another time a mean boy at the Country Buffet made Benny trip and drop his food and called him a dummy. Benny hated him. He couldn't stop thinking about how much he hated the mean boy sitting two tables away. He stared at him while they ate. And then it happened. The boy grabbed his throat like he couldn't breathe. The boy's father shouted and squeezed his son hard from the back and the boy barfed all over the table. At first it made Benny happy. But after a while it gave him an icky feeling. He decided he didn't like being mean, even when he had a good reason.

The bad man shooting at Dad was a good reason, but Benny had a better idea.

He would have to take off his motorcycle

helmet so his thoughts could get out. He struggled to unbuckle the strap. Usually Dad or Grace helped him. The harder he tried, the clumsier his fingers got. The heat made him feel weak and he wanted to give up. Tears pushed at the corners of his eyes.

You can't cry! Dad needs you! Stop being a baby!

Benny made himself concentrate and slow down, like Dad always told him to do, and the buckle let go. He pulled the helmet off and ran his fingers through his short, damp hair. The air felt good. He hung his helmet off the motorcycle's handlebar. The sun burned the top of his head so he untied his pirate hat from its place above the headlight and put it on, making sure it rested low in front to shade his eyes. It wasn't as thick as the helmet so his thoughts would be able to get through okay.

He sat cross-legged in the shade of the bike, closed his eyes tight and pictured his dad in his mind. Tall and strong. Not strong like the Terminator, but strong like rope. He had short brown hair, like Benny's, but with lots of gray. His blue eyes were smart and true and had the knowing of a lot of things. His smile warmed Benny's insides like hot rolls fresh from the oven.

Mama called him handsome.

Benny's mind wandered at the thought of his mama. He missed her. He missed her hugs. He missed her "nighty night, sleep tight." He missed her fried chicken. He hurt inside sometimes, he missed her so bad.

But he didn't have time to think about Mama right now. He had to help Dad. He imagined a movie screen in his head and saw Dad running. Faster and faster, Benny pictured his long legs flying like he had wings on his feet.

Run, Dad! Run like the wind blows!

He repeated it. *Run, Dad!* But it didn't feel right. Benny remembered how fast the car moved and he knew his dad couldn't run fast enough, no matter how hard he wanted it to be so. He might not be the smartest boy in town, but he knew that much. He changed his message.

Get down, Dad! He's coming! Get small!

Benny heard another shot. He squeezed his eyes so tight it made his face hurt. He sent the message again and again.

Get down! Get small!

A giant bird – an eagle – flew into his thoughts. He didn't know where it came from. It dived, then went up high, its wings spread wide. Benny felt its strength. Its courage. He felt the wind on its face. It turned its head to look down and Benny realized he could see what it saw, like he was inside the eagle, looking through its big yellow eyes. He saw a man staring up at them. Daddy. The eagle told Benny it would keep his daddy safe. Then it gave a squeaky cackle, and Benny opened his eyes. He felt calm inside because he knew he did all he could.

He rolled to his hands and knees, then straightened his stiff legs and pushed his butt into the air. He popped off a fart that sounded funny through his leather pants. A popcorn fart, his dad would call it. Benny giggled.

He stood and a shiver went through him. He'd seen this place before, in the movies. Thelma and Louise drove through here. John Wayne. The Lone Ranger. It made him feel small, but not in a bad way. If he listened really hard, he could hear the rock walls sing to him. Soft, beautiful words he didn't know, over and over. Chanting. He remembered watching a TV show with Mama about Indians that lived in cliffs just like these years and years ago. He heard the beat of a drum. Then many drums. *This place is magic.* He looked to the ridges, expecting to see Indians watching, but that only happened in the movies.

When he looked back down, he saw something a ways away that didn't seem like it should be there. He squinted at it for a long time. It looked like the roof of a house.

~~~

Grace realized the foolishness of her attempt to shield Benny when the sidecar jolted the air from her lungs and she popped up like a cork from a champagne bottle. The sidecar went on without her and the desert floor came at her fast. She pulled into a ball and hit the ground ass over tea kettle, rolled once then felt the earth drop away. She gave a startled scream that ended on a grunt when she jarred to a stop at the bottom of a short embankment.

She listened to the fading rumble of the motorcycle. "Lord have mercy, they done gone on without me." Dazed, she looked back at the rocky embankment – about a four-foot drop – and marveled that she hadn't injured more than just her dignity with her unplanned launch and flight. The only damage to her person, besides a bruised backside, appeared to be a scuff on the right forearm of her leather jacket. Her rugged riding attire had protected her.

She snorted. "Get real, honey. Your fat

behind saved you."

A scrub jay scolded her from its perch in a nearby juniper, bobbing its head as it watched, curious over the strange creature that had invaded its territory.

Grace could only imagine the sight she must have made, an overweight sister in helmet and leathers tumbling across the desert floor. She laughed and the scrub jay flew off with a disgruntled squawk. Brushing at the dust on her knees, Grace wondered what Eddy would say if he could see her now.

~~~

The headline – *Stardust Casino Sees Last Roll of Dice* – ignited a memory so startling, Grace sucked in a sharp breath.

"Bad news?" her husband asked from across the breakfast table.

Every Sunday morning they hauled their old bones out of bed extra early, ate a bowl of warm steel cut oats with raisins, downed a pot of coffee, and read the paper together before church services. Ed said it helped take his mind off the sermon he had to give.

Grace stared at the headline, unable to find her voice. *I forgot about the Stardust.*

At seventy-one, memory lapses beset her: leaving for the market without her grocery list, misplacing keys, walking into a room and not knowing why. Things most people, including her husband, shrugged off as normal for her age. But she knew better. Doctor Medford – when she pressed him for an answer – confirmed her heightened risk of developing dementia because of family history. He called her memory blips mild panic attacks. "You need to relax," he advised. "Worrying only compounds the problem." Relax? She was the same age her papa had been when grief stole his mind. He died a starved man, hungering to taste the lifetime of memories just out of his grasp.

But to his last breath, he remembered the Stardust and the civil rights milestone it represented. He marched through the front doors of that casino and declared, *Liberty! Freedom! Tyranny is dead!* Papa always did have a flair for the dramatic; Shakespeare's *Julius Caesar* being a favorite of his.

"Gracie, what is it? You look like you've seen a ghost."

She studied the historical photo accompanying the headline: Earth, circled by a satellite ring and flanked by stars and planets, loomed over the entrance of the casino. A ghost from the past. Her past. *How could I forget? How am I supposed to relax?*

She lifted her gaze to her husband. He looked fine in his dark gray windowpane suit, the richness of his deep bronze skin enhanced by his ivory shirt and his snowy hair clipped close. The purple tie he wore complimented the purple and ivory swirl pattern of her shantung petal jacket and flared dress. It pleased him to compliment her style, he reminded her often. She dearly loved her man but knew he would downplay her memory fade as nothing to worry about. Forgetting the Stardust unsettled her too much to be made light of.

"Must be this awful heat," she finally said.

Concern plowed Ed's forehead. "Maybe you should stay home today, honey."

"Lord have mercy, no. The sisters'd be rushin' over after church to fuss on me."

"Uh huh. The widow Boucher makes a mean macaroni and cheese casserole," he said with a straight face.

Grace sniffed and Ed's deep laugh boomed off the walls of the breakfast nook. Elsie Boucher had been attending United Christian Methodist longer than any other member of the congregation, including the preacher and his wife. She had a memory that defied her closely guarded age, and in all those un-numbered years the woman still couldn't cook a decent casserole to save her soul.

"Are you sure you're okay?" Ed asked.

Grace's heart tightened. When a handsome preacher-man name of Edward Brown showed up regular at the diner where she waited tables – because he liked the way she poured his coffee – she told him about her papa, a year in his grave by then, how he'd been a professional poker player and how she played alongside him once she got grown. "I thought you should know," she said, "'fore you get any notions about asking me to marry you. Something like that gets out, it could look bad on your reputation."

"Do you still gamble?" he asked.

"No. I couldn't keep my emotions out of it anymore. Those days are behind me."

"That suits me fine."

It suited Grace too. She accepted his proposal and devoted the next forty years to being a wife, mother, and active member of the church. The stories she told of her papa, Charlie James, faded over time, pushed into the recesses of her memory by the needs of living in the present day-to-day. What if she lost those stories of the past for good? What, or who, would she forget next? Ed? Their children? Brother Joe?

Grace's hands shook a bit as she folded the newspaper and smoothed the crease. The battery-operated clock above the stove ticked with methodic persistence while her husband waited for an answer.

Straightening, she pushed her chair back, said, "I'll be fine," and stood before Ed could reply. She reached for her purple Kentucky Derby straw hat with its up-turned wide brim, large milk-white silk roses and sheer organza ribbon. "We need to go. You don't never like to be late for churching."

~~~

Grace heard the car approach. She stilled and prayed she couldn't be seen from above. She'd had her fill of the distasteful little man she knew to be driving.

The car didn't slow as it headed in Ray and Benny's direction.

Please, Lord Jesus alive, keep them two safe.

When the sound died away, Grace scrambled to the top of the embankment and removed her helmet. The canyon extended forever in all directions, sandstone formations in vivid shades of rust and umber and fire, precarious spires at the mercy of erosion. Spiky agave and yucca dotted the landscape with green. Heat shimmered off the red dust and an untamed energy pulsed in the air. It stirred the quarter Cherokee blood that pumped through her veins.

The terrain reminded her of the Navajo reservation, one of many detours Papa took them on while traveling from game to game. He wanted his children to experience the culture and history of a native people with roots that mirrored their own. Much of her and Joe's education had come from the road. "Better than any book-learnin'," Papa told them. Standing in this rugged place made the sweet ache of missing him and brother Joe palpable.

The high desert sky stretched as wide and endless as the canyon, an unchanging azure canopy. Grace drew in a long breath and let it fill her lungs. They didn't have air like this in Little Rock. A lone Bald Eagle rode the thermals. Grace watched as it tucked its wings and dove in the direction the motorcycle had gone. She saw a low dust cloud dissipating in the distance.

I need to find them boys.

The sharp report of a gunshot echoed up the canyon. Grace yelped, "Lord have mercy!" and took off running toward the sound as fast as she could make her stiff muscles and heavy motorcycle boots move.

2: Fried Chicken

"Son, what's taking so long?" Ray called through the closed bedroom door. "My feet are itchin' to leave."

"'kay, Dad."

The door opened and Ray tried his damnedest to keep from cracking up. Benny wore a god-awful orange, pink and green Hawaiian print shirt over his camouflage cargo shorts, the pockets bulging like saddlebags, and a pair of black and white checkered deck shoes with the sides blown out.

Why does he still have those? Ray wondered, staring at the shoes. Virginia bought them for their son...when? Two summers ago? How the hell did he manage to get his feet into them?

Ray looked up. An Instamatic camera that

hadn't worked in years hung around Benny's neck by a narrow strap, almost lost in the loose folds of the wild, over-sized shirt. A shirt Ray had never seen before. He would have remembered. *What happened to the one I put on the bed for him?*

He thought of all the reasons he shouldn't let his boy leave the house dressed like that, and settled for, "Change your shoes, son."

"Oh, man."

Ray had packed his son's clothes, then left the suitcase open for Benny to add whatever personal stuff he wanted to take. Apparently that included his custom orthopedic sneakers. It didn't surprise Ray that Benny managed to zip the case shut on his own and wrestle it out to the car. The boy was strong for his age.

Ray popped the trunk of his '69 Oldsmobile 442 Cutlass and reached under the two new sleeping bags for Benny's bulging suitcase. When he got it open, he found the shirt he'd laid out, now neatly folded around the 5 x 7 framed photograph of Virginia that Benny kept on his nightstand. She stood waist deep in tomato plants, the sleeves of her white blouse rolled to her elbows and a wide-brimmed straw hat shading her face. She loved that vegetable garden. She looked up when Ray called her name from the edge of the fence and the sun caught her face. *Oh you,* she said, but smiled, and he snapped the picture.

A surge of grief knocked the air from Ray's lungs. For long seconds, he leaned against the car's chrome bumper, his knees locked to keep from collapsing, and stared into his wife's eyes. She was too far away for the camera to pick it up, but he knew their pale green by heart. He remembered her laughter when he told her they reminded him of the ferns that grew wild in the forest. *Are you getting poetic on me, Ray Colton?* And then she gave herself to him for the first time.

Ray traced his finger down the image of her cheek, the glass cool to his touch. Like her skin had been that morning.

Why didn't I wake up?

"God damn it," he said, drawing his anger through him like a hot blade. He took care to rewrap the photo and put it back where he found it. He pulled Benny's shoes out, zipped the suitcase and shoved it under the sleeping bags.

He noticed the fishing gear pushed deep into the rear of the trunk. Benny must have hauled it from the garage. Just like Thelma in the movie, his son packed the gear even

28

though he had never been fishing. Two collapsible trout rods, the lines rotted and tangled, the tackle box with a jar of roe that could be a science project, the fishing vest Ray's dad gave him years ago. Benny even managed to get the net down from its hook high on the garage wall.

Ray decided they would camp their way across the states. He and Benny set up the four-man dome tent in the back yard two days ago to let it air out and check for damage. It smelled musty, but otherwise looked in good shape. Karen must have been five or six years old when Ray bought it. The three of them used it twice as a family — a trip to Cumberland Gap and another to Mammoth Caves National Park. Virginia didn't care for sleeping on the ground, heating wash water, cooking from coolers. Said it was more work than relaxation. After that, Ray and Karen tented a handful of times, just the two of them, mostly overnight fishing trips. But then his daughter became more interested in boys than fish and the tent got packed away in the attic.

The tent stayed packed away after Benny came along. Whenever Ray suggested taking their son camping, Virginia rattled off a list of reasons not to. "You know how susceptible he is to respiratory infections." "You know how scared he is of crawly things. What if a spider walks across his face in the middle of the night?" "What if a bear wanders into camp?"

Ray gave up.

Not anymore, he vowed, closing the trunk lid. Maybe Gin was right, but he needed to find out for himself.

Karen had done her best to change his mind. She invited them over for a bon voyage dinner yesterday evening and asked, "Are you sure this is a good idea, Dad?" as she handed him the bowl of mashed potatoes. Her husband, Evan, sat at the other end of the table within reach of their two-year-old, blue-eyed twins, Jeffery and Jacob. Grandpa and Uncle Benny sat across from them. Karen had put a gob of potatoes and gravy on each boy's plate, and the duo already wore it in their hair and down the front of their Garanimals.

Ray would miss the little goobers.

"It's just a vacation," he said, taking the bowl from her. He tried to sound convincing as he plopped a mound of potatoes on his plate, then gave Benny some. Benny groaned in protest when Ray passed the bowl on to Evan. "Eat what's on your plate first," Ray told him. He'd learned the hard way not to let Benny serve himself. The boy's eyes were bigger than his stomach and he'd eat himself sick if given half a chance.

Karen handed him the gravy boat. "What if something happens?" she asked. "Benny's never been that far away from home. You don't even own a cell phone."

The cell phone again. He had no use for one. He figured that's what pay phones were for. "We'll be fine."

"I know, but it's just so soon after Mama's..."

Ray looked up and saw the unfinished sentence on his daughter's face. At that moment, with her shoulder-length brown hair pulled back in a ponytail, she looked more like his little girl than a twenty-three-year-old mother of two. He realized it wasn't that she didn't think he could manage Benny in an unfamiliar environment. She was afraid of losing her daddy on the heels of her mama's passing.

"Don't worry, pumpkin. We'll check in once we're down the road a ways."

"You better." She thrust a plate of fried chicken at him. "Eat up. Goodness knows when you'll get another home-cooked meal."

Benny covered his mouth to hide his giggle.

"And you, Mister Smarty Pants, you behave

31

yourself and take care of our daddy."

"'kay, honey."

~~~

As Ray pulled out of the driveway, Benny riding shotgun in the front bucket seat, he glanced in the rearview mirror and said a silent goodbye to the yellow ranch-style house he and Virginia called home for twenty-five years. The home where they raised their two children. The home where she died. Regret and relief warred with his conscience. He wondered when he'd see the house again. Did he want to?

He didn't have a planned route, his only agenda to get out of Ohio as fast as legally possible. Once he made the decision three days ago to take his son to the Grand Canyon, leaving became his sole focus. He washed laundry, gave the Olds an oil change, put a hold on mail delivery, canceled the newspaper, and asked Karen to keep her mama's tomatoes watered. When she wanted to know why the big hurry, he told her "summer break's already half over," for lack of a better explanation.

He could have headed west on I-70, but flat, humid Indiana held about as much appeal as a boil on his ass. He pointed the Olds south, taking I-675 out of Beavercreek, and connected with I-75 through Cincinnati. He drove like a man with demons on his tail, windows down, oppressive heat blasting across the white vinyl interior of the car. The Olds didn't have air conditioning, a fact Virginia reminded him of, often. The Burgundy Mist 442 with white hood stripes and W-30 engine option was one of the few things he stood his ground on. He bought the muscle car new off a lot in Dayton, Ohio, after getting out of the Air Force, and drove it all the way to Oregon to see his folks.

His Smith & Wesson .357 magnum revolver with six-inch barrel — something else Virginia frowned on him having — was loaded and locked in the glove box.

Ray drove one-handed, his left elbow resting on the window frame, wind tugging at the sleeve of his white t-shirt. Benny mirrored the pose from the passenger's bucket seat, his short arm jutting up at what looked like an uncomfortable angle. His traffic-stopper shirt billowed around the weight of the camera strap like a colorful banner. He pulled a pair of Terminator sunglasses from a side pocket of his cargo shorts, said "*Hasta la vista,* baby," as he put them on. Or words to that effect. Ray had seen the movie enough times to know what the boy meant.

He glanced over at Benny and smiled. His son looked like any kid on vacation. It yanked at his heart. He drove with the single-minded purpose of making up for lost time. The 360-horsepower Ram Air V-8 gobbled miles and gas with the precision of a fine watch; the dual exhausts purred with authority.

They crossed the jagged Ohio River into Kentucky — home of Daniel Boone, Loretta Lynn and Colonel Harland Sanders, the founder of Kentucky Fried Chicken — when Benny said, "Dad?"

"What, son?"

"I gotta pee."

They'd been on the road for a little over an hour. "Didn't you go before we left the house?" Ray asked, unwilling to lose momentum.

"I forgot," Benny mumbled.

Ray took a deep breath, let it out slow. "Okay then."

They stopped at a rest area just outside Florence and hit the road again in less than five minutes. Ray pushed the Olds to the speed limit, bulleting through tree-lined corridors, trying to make up pee-break minutes. He stayed on I-75, headed south toward Lexington. The bluegrass region of Kentucky rolled out from the Interstate in a green, lush carpet of farmland behind long wooden fences. Transparent clouds popcorned a flat, blue sky. The air smelled washed.

Before reaching Lexington, they stopped at another rest area. Then in town, Ray pulled into a gas station, bought coffee and a road atlas while Benny went pee a third time.

When his son came out of the rest room, Ray asked, "Do you really have a squirrel bladder? Or are you just afraid there won't be another bathroom for hundreds of miles?"

"Yeah, Dad."

"That's what I thought."

~~~

Benny was glad his dad didn't get mad about all the bathroom stops. He was glad he didn't have to worry because "the world is full of places to go pee." Daddy was good at explaining things.

They would head west for a while, Daddy said, to Elizabethtown, then go south some more. Benny pretended to be interested, but he didn't really care as long as they got to the Grand Canyon. He liked the feel of the hot air blowing his shirt off his skin when they drove fast. His Terminator sunglasses made everything dark and cool. The trees and horses and big white barns looked neat, and the air smelled green. But mostly he watched his dad's color halo get brighter. He peeked over the top of his sunglasses to be sure, then smiled inside.

He couldn't always see the colors, and sometimes he saw them when he didn't want to. Like when Mama got sick. Her color halo got dark and muddy. Benny knew something was wrong but he didn't know what to do about it. And then Mama died. She died because he was stupid and didn't know how to help her.

When he saw Daddy's color halo get dark, it worried him. It worried him a lot. He didn't like the way his dad sat on the couch every day and stared at the TV without seeing it. Benny knew that look. Strangers looked at him that way, like he wasn't even there. That's how his dad watched TV.

Except it was different with Thelma and Louise. When their car flew like an eagle over the Grand Canyon at the end of the movie, Daddy had a wanting look in his eyes. It gave Benny an idea. His ideas mostly turned out to be dumb, but this one was good. It had to be. He wasn't going to let Daddy die.

Benny's stomach rumbled and he checked his scuba-diver watch, the one Mama bought him for his birthday because he kept getting his other watch wet and it stopped working. "Dad?"

"What, son?"

"Time for lunch."

~~~

Ray spotted a Wendy's in Elizabethtown and they stopped for bacon cheeseburgers and fries. Benny ordered root beer and Ray chugged the largest coffee they had. One more pee call – "Squirrel bladder," Ray teased, making Benny giggle – and they got back on the road. Ray picked up I-65 and headed south for the Kentucky-Tennessee border. Two hours later, the caffeine wore off. Fatigue fogged his concentration, and getting through Nashville took all the steam out of him. A lot of years had passed since he'd driven any kind of stretch at one time. He could feel the miles in every bone of his body. An hour west of Nashville, on I-40, he saw a KOA campground and pulled in.

"What'd'ya say we call this home for the night?" he asked, parking in front of the main lodge.

Benny slid his sunglasses down his nose and looked around. "Nice."

Ray paid for a site — a shaded, level spot

among evergreens and sheltering shrubs. Benny helped him set up the tent. They spread out their sleeping bags and the boy flopped on his back in the middle of them. "C'mon, Dad. It's good."

It did look good. Comfortable. Ray dared to hope it might be enough to break his spell of sleeplessness. "Don't be going to bed on me yet," he said. "We haven't had dinner."

"Oh yeah!" Benny shot up and scrambled for the door. The side pocket of his cargo shorts caught the edge of the tent opening and yanked the frame askew. Ray held his breath, expecting the whole thing to pull free of its stakes. Then the cargo pocket let go and Benny barreled toward him head first, arms flailing.

Ray caught and steadied him. "Slow down there. You goin' to a fire?"

"No, dinner."

"I saw a restaurant over that way." Ray put an arm around his son's shoulders and pointed through the trees. "Let's take us a little walk, go see if they have anything good on the menu."

Benny patted his stomach. "Fried chicken?"

"I wouldn't be surprised."

~~~

The flicker of campfires and the smell of wood smoke greeted them when they returned to their site, their bellies full of fried chicken and mashed potatoes. Crickets tuned up for an evening chorus and the low murmuring of other campers filtered through the shrubs. Ray got the battery-operated lantern from the trunk. He and Benny made a final trip to the restroom, then dragged their suitcases inside the tent and zipped the door. The close confines and remaining heat of the day pressed in on them. Ray opened the flaps over the screened windows for cross ventilation. He removed his Dr. Scholl's slip-ons and set them at the end of his sleeping bag. Benny watched, did the same with his sneakers. Ray squirmed out of his jeans like a caterpillar on its back. Benny tried a different approach and stuck his butt in Ray's face.

"Whoa! Watch where you point that thing."

Benny giggled. "Sorry."

"Yeah, well, just make sure it don't go off."

"'kay, Dad." Benny sat and gave his cargo shorts a final yank, freeing them of his squat legs.

Ray rolled his jeans and put them at the head of his sleeping bag.

"Uh?" Benny's eyes went wide. "Pillows?"

"I had to forget something, didn't I?"

Benny released a dramatic sigh, a trait he

picked up from his mama. "Yeah." He set about emptying the pockets of his cargo shorts. Sunglasses. Lip balm. Wallet. A wad of keys, most of which didn't go to anything. A small box of crayons and a pocket-size packet of tissues. He took off his waterproof watch and removed the camera from around his neck, added them to the collection, then methodically arranged everything in a neat row next to his sleeping bag.

Ray rolled the boy's cargo shorts into a makeshift pillow for him. "Don't sleep in that shirt, son. It'll give me nightmares."

"'kay."

Benny tugged his suitcase onto the foot of his sleeping bag and almost bopped Ray in the eye with his elbow. "Sorry," he mumbled. He pulled out his Terminator t-shirt. "This?"

"That one's fine."

Benny closed his suitcase and pushed it off to the side. He changed out of his Hawaiian shirt, then waved it around as though not sure what to do with it.

Ray felt like telling him to toss it out the door. "Lay it on top of your suitcase," he said, and slid into his sleeping bag.

"'kay, Dad."

Benny climbed into his own sleeping bag

and Ray finally asked, "Son, where'd you get that shirt?"

"Aunt Georgie."

Virginia's sister Georgia. Crazy as a loon, as far as Ray was concerned. Probably on her way to her third afternoon cocktail when she bought the ugly thing. Which would explain why Virginia kept it hidden from him. "You ready to have the light off?" he asked.

"Yeah."

Ray reached for the lantern switch.

"Dad?"

"What is it?"

"If I need to go pee..."

"Wake me and I'll go with you."

"'kay."

"Good night then."

"Night, Dad."

Ray turned off the light.

~~~

Darth Vader is chasing Princess Leia and she's screaming for help! I grab my lightsaber. Darth Vader stops and turns. He has his lightsaber and tries to hit me with it. I swing mine at him but I miss. I swing again and hit something. I hear a crash and see the broken pieces of Mama's favorite vase, the tall blue and white one that her daddy bought for her in Germany. She calls it Dresden.

Mama yells, "What was that?" I can't move. I did a bad thing and my body is frozen. Mama comes into the room and sees what I did. "No! How many times have I told you not to swing that broom handle in the house?" She starts to cry. "Look what you've done."

"I'll fix it," I tell her. I start to cry too because I know there's too many pieces.

Mama gets an angry look on her face. "You can't fix it!" she shouts and goes to her bedroom and shuts the door.

I can't fix it because I'm a stupid boy. I pick up one of the pieces but it cuts my finger and I drop it. Stupid boy! I hate being stupid! Slap. *I can't do anything right.* Slap.

Somebody is shaking me. "Wake up, son." Daddy's voice. "Stop hitting yourself. Son, wake up."

Benny opened his eyes.

Daddy had the light turned on. "Bad dream?"

It wasn't a dream. He broke Mama's Dresden vase and she got really mad and then she cried and her color halo got bad and he didn't say anything because he was a stupid boy and she died. Benny tried to tell his dad but the words came too fast and he couldn't make them sound right.

"Slow down, son. You're getting yourself all worked up."

Benny tried again but the words wouldn't come. His face hurt. Frustrated, he started to cry for real.

Daddy hugged him close. "Just relax."

It felt good to have Daddy hug him, but it wasn't the same as Mama's hugs. Mama had soft places and she smelled like flowers. Benny knew he would never feel her hugs again and it made him cry more.

~~~

Ray knew about the vase and Virginia's anger. She'd gotten angry with their son before, of course. It always blew over. But after the vase incident, Ray would catch Benny watching his mama with an odd look, almost like he saw something the rest of them didn't.

Three weeks later, Virginia died and the boy's nightmares began. Ray thought they had something to do with the vase but he hadn't been able to piece together enough of the boy's rants to be sure. The slapping concerned him. Benny often resorted to slapping his face when he got frustrated and couldn't make people understand. But in his nightmares the slapping became violent.

Ray felt helpless to comfort his son. The boy

needed his mama to tell him things were okay; but things weren't okay because Virginia passed away in her sleep, leaving Benny and him to go on without her. Ray cursed her for that, knowing it didn't make sense because it wasn't something she had any control over. He cursed her and he cursed himself for not realizing there was anything wrong as she slept beside him.

Benny drifted back to sleep, his hot skin damp against Ray's shoulder. The soft nasal sounds he made as he breathed with his mouth open chorused the crickets outside the tent. Silent tears slid hot down Ray's face.

3: Full Tilt

Grace fanned herself with the church bulletin as the ceiling fans twirled lethargic and helpless against Little Rock's August heat. An insufferable concoction of perfumes, after shaves, lemon furniture wax and dust collided with the smell of too many over-heated bodies and their failed deodorants all packed into a confined space. It hurt to breathe. She focused on her loving husband's tall, commanding presence at the pulpit, tried to concentrate on the sermon she must have heard a dozen times. The cadence of his voice flowed through her head like blackstrap molasses, dulling her ability to pay attention. "God will supply every need," she heard him say. *Then why ain't we praying for an air conditioning unit?*

She cast her gaze across the pews of familiar

faces, an ethnic stewpot that spoke well of the reverend's popularity. Stella, her copper penny complexion complimented by an animal print and beadwork cloche hat, sat next to her latest beau, a scandalous fifteen years her junior. Roberta and Stanley looked frazzled around the edges, their five sandy-haired children in tow, all dressed in homemade coordinating pastel cottons. The youngest, dear six-year-old Anna, had Down syndrome. Will and his Japanese-American wife, Mei, the newest members of the church, their two beautiful, light brown babies both still in diapers, sat near the back in case they needed to hustle out with a fussy one. The widow Boucher, vibrant in a crimson church suit and matching hat with a brim so wide it nearly sliced the side of poor Mr. Stuart's neck every time she turned her head. Mr. Stuart, a quiet, tolerant man, arrived pallid and alone that morning, his fool wife home recovering from a toe she broke while gardening. How on earth the woman managed to break her toe was anybody's guess.

Ed's younger sister, Arleeta, stunning in her powder blue suit and matching sinamay derby with feather bouquet and over-sized bow, also sat spouseless, her husband, Harold, no doubt at home glued to the TV. Grace had little tolerance for the man, but he was a good provider, and he put up with his wife's constant chirping better than most.

Grace knew each parishioner like family, yet this morning she felt isolated. She didn't talk about her gambling days in church. How could she expect any of these people to understand her heartbreak over some ol' casino she forgot? To her knowing, not a one of them believed she be losing her mind. *Don't trouble yourself, sister. Everybody forgets things from time to time. You're makin' a fuss over nothing.*

In spite of the heat and her shantung jacket with its three-quarter sleeves, a chill shivered over her shoulders and down her arms. If only she could breathe.

The congregation rose to their feet in a cacophony of thumps and rustling and throat clearing as they prepared to sing. The flower-petal hem of Grace's knee-length skirt clung to the back of her sweaty thighs. She gave a discrete tug, then fixed her eyes on the massive wooden cross on the wall behind the pulpit.

"'I am weak but Thou art strong,'" she sang in a loud, clear voice. Her papa had loved to hear her sing. Even after he lost interest in living, she could make him smile with "The Man I Love" and "Summertime."

"'Jesus, keep me from all wrong,'" she continued. Right or wrong, Papa drank in life like a man dying of thirst — big, impatient gulps. The day he took his daughter through the front entrance of the Stardust casino and sat at a gaming table with white folk for the first time, head high and shoulders back, he said his how-do-you-do's, anted up and won enough in that single day to feed them for a month. Amen.

"'I'll be satisfied as long...'"

Tears welled in her eyes and her voice faded. She ached to relive that moment, to stroll through the Stardust and see her papa sitting proud and playing the game he loved. In a few days it would all be nothing but a pile of forgotten rubble.

I'd like to see it one last time.

She dug a tissue from the side pocket of her purse. Her hand trembled as she wiped at her eyes and damp forehead. "'Who with me my burden shares?'" the rest of the congregation sang, already on the second verse. "'None but Thee, my dear Lord, none but Thee.'"

Grace doubted even the Lord shared the burden she struggled under. She felt disconnected, her life fraying.

Pull yourself together. Everybody's starin' at

you.

She drew her back straight and picked up the hymn mid-sentence. "'...closer walk with Thee! Jesus, grant — '" Her mind went blank. *Grant what?*

The congregation sang on but their words didn't make any sense, an unintelligible drone in her ringing ears. Fear iced through her. She tried to draw in a breath but her lungs constricted against the assault of smells. Darkness narrowed her vision.

Lord Jesus, I'm going to faint.

Air. I need air.

"Excuse me," she mouthed to Mrs. Turner sitting on her left. Gladys Turner gave her a tart-lemon look but squeezed back against the pew to let Grace by.

Mr. Turner was a big man with feet to match. Grace managed to plant the heel of her white pump square on the top of his size thirteen wingtip. She knew he wore a size thirteen because his wife never missed an opportunity to remind members of the Ladies' Social Club what a time she had finding clothes to fit her "mountain of a man."

Grace muttered "sorry" to the mountain and reached the aisle at the far left of the sanctuary. Darting through the side exit as though headed for the restroom, she hugged her purse to her bosom and did a green-apple-quick-step down the narrow, beige hall, past classrooms, the choir room and the pastor's office. She passed the restroom without slowing and reached for the exit.

Heat robbed her breath as the solid metal door clicked shut behind her. Sun-baked blacktop replaced the smell of perspiring bodies. Grace paused on the concrete landing, gripped the railing to keep from pitching over the edge, and squinted against the glare of chrome and windshields. *I want to go home.* She located their yellow-cream Lincoln in the parking lot, and began to dig in her purse for the keys as she made her way down the short flight of steps. Ed can get a ride home from his sister, she thought, as she passed Arleeta's sporty steel-blue Honda. Harold bought it from Bob's Best Deals six months ago so his wife could drive to church in style. Grace rode in the car many times, even drove it once when Arleeta over-indulged at a church potluck and feared throwing up on the steering wheel. It fit Grace perfect. And it had air conditioning.

The keys dangled from the ignition, the driver's-side door unlocked. "Leeta, Leeta," Grace scolded, "how many times have I warned you?"

She dug deeper in her purse for the keys to the Lincoln. Sweat snaked down her back and her hands shook as she tore through pockets, hoping she put the ring in the wrong place. The longer she stood in the hot sun, the more urgent her need to flee before she passed out. She pulled her house keys from her purse, hoping they had tangled with the car keys. She'd read somewhere that it was best to keep the two rings separate but couldn't recall why. If the keys were on the same ring, she'd be halfway home by now. What good did it do her to be able to get into the house if she couldn't get to the house? Her chest tightened.

What's wrong with me? Am I having a heart attack?

The forgotten lyrics came to her. *Jesus, grant my humble plea.* She felt her eyes drawn to Arleeta's car sitting unlocked, key in the ignition.

Not one to question fate nor Jesus, Grace hustled over and got in.

~~~

Somewhere on the drive from church to home, Grace made up her mind to go to Las Vegas and see the Stardust before there was no Stardust to see. Before she could forget it ever existed. Before she ran out of time. She threw clothes into a dusty suitcase she dragged from the closet and grabbed her rainy-day stash from the heart-shaped Valentine's box at the back of her lingerie drawer. She didn't need to count it, knew there was exactly $374. Enough to get her to Vegas.

Was it enough to get her back home?

The Lord will provide. Go!

Grace jerked as if goosed, hooked her purse over her arm, grabbed the suitcase and headed for the door. Once outside, she tossed the suitcase in the Honda's trunk and reached to close the lid.

You can't take sister's car.

A cab. I'll call a cab.

Grace yanked the suitcase from the trunk and lumbered back up the porch, went to open the door before remembering she had locked it. The pointed end of a nail file stabbed her little finger as she dug through her purse for the keys. A dirt-encrusted lemon lozenge stuck to the side of her hand. She found a tube of Cranberry Glaze lipstick with a white hair caught in the cap, but no keys. Her skin prickled with cold sweat and it crossed her mind that she hadn't packed any toiletries.

"Jesus, help me," Grace groaned. She

grabbed the doorknob and gave it a violent twist, but the door didn't budge. The kitchen phone began to ring. A dark fog clouded her brain.

I'm running out of time.

She stumbled down the porch steps in her rush back to Arleeta's car, threw her suitcase into the trunk and slammed the lid. Climbing behind the wheel, she drove.

~~~

Traffic demands helped focus Grace's jumbled thoughts as she left Little Rock, headed west on I-40. The Honda's AC cooled her sweat-dampened skin and eased the tightness in her chest. "I've got money," she reasoned aloud. "I can buy deodorant, hair products, a toothbrush. I'll get a nice hotel room in Vegas and use their little soaps. I'll be fine."

I'll be fine as long as my money holds out. I've never spent the night in a Vegas hotel. What does a room cost? For that matter, what does a bus ticket cost?

She'd know soon enough. The bus depot in Conway was about a half hour from Little Rock. Once she bought her ticket, she would call home and let Ed know where to pick up his sister's car.

What will I say to him?

"Sorry I stole Leeta's car, but I'm on my way to Vegas and losing my mind."

The tightness in her chest returned. *Have mercy upon me, O God.*

Conway came into view. *I need more distance.* Punching on the radio, Grace accelerated and shot past the exit, accompanied by Dinah Washington singing a familiar tune about change. Grace sang along as the car ate highway. The louder she sang, the easier it got to block out the voice telling her to turn around.

A tractor-trailer rig passed in the left lane. Grace stopped singing and waited for the truck to merge in front of her. When it did, she heard a sharp *whap* from the front of the car and flinched. Thinking one of the truck's tires might have pitched road debris at her, she glanced at the hood of the car, then checked the highway in the rearview mirror, but didn't see anything out of the ordinary.

The smell of hot rubber curled in her nostrils. She shut off the radio, as though that would make it easier to identify the smell's source. As the truck became a dot on the horizon, the smell grew stronger. Grace drove on, praying it was nothing, her palms sweaty on the steering wheel in spite of the AC. She had the fleeting thought she should have let daughter Luella buy her that cell phone. Smoke began rolling from under the hood.

"Lord have mercy!" Grace quickly pulled to the side of the Interstate, stopped and reached for the key. The engine gave a sonic *BANG*. Grace screamed; the car shuddered and died.

A white cloud engulfed the front of the car. She stared at it dumbfounded for a few seconds, her heart pounding against her chest wall.

Fire, you fool! Get out!

4: The First Rescue

Ray hoped to reach the Oklahoma border by mid-afternoon as he pushed the throttle of the Olds west on I-40 Sunday morning. He and Benny had stowed the camping gear in the trunk, then filled their bellies on biscuits and sausage gravy at the same restaurant they walked to the evening before. Ray could almost hear Virginia complaining about the salty meal and how she'd be bloated for the rest of the day. He and Benny would exchange a look and start snickering. Virginia would flutter her hand at them, "Oh, you two," and join in. The memory left a deep ache in its place.

The day didn't waste any time turning up the thermostat. Ray made it his mission to get through it as fast as possible. Benny slept sound after his nightmare, but sleep continued to elude Ray, leaving him more frustrated and on edge than ever. Powered by adrenaline and a gallon of coffee, he plowed through the floodplains of the Mississippi River, where heat, humidity, and miles of flat land made cotton and soybeans ideal crops. Benny had repacked the pockets of his cargo shorts and put his wild Hawaiian shirt back on. Wearing his Terminator sunglasses, he rode shotgun with his head out the window, chin thrust into the hot air. Ray smiled to himself and pressed the throttle down a fraction more.

From the Interstate, Memphis was just another city to get through. Business districts. High-rises. Benny snapped pictures of a steel and glass pyramid structure with his empty camera as they started across the wide, flat Mississippi River and into Arkansas. They covered more miles of flat and farmland, interspersed with tree- and brush-lined corridors. Ray figured the greenery was intended to contain the noise and grime from the Interstate. It sure made for a lot of boring sameness. Church bells rang the noon hour as they bought burgers and fries, root beer and more coffee in North Little Rock. They ate on the fly, staying on I-40, headed west.

Ray felt like he might never stop driving, just keep his foot on the throttle until they reached the Oregon Coast and had to start swimming. He didn't want to know where the feeling came from. Distance. That's what he focused on. Distance and speed. There'd be time to sort the reasons once he felt like he'd gone far enough and could —

"Look out, Dad!"

Ray jerked his attention back to his driving and saw a car door swing open in front of them. Too close. Too fast. "Hang on!" he shouted and yanked the steering wheel a hard left.

The rear leaf-spring suspension and stabilizer bar held the car on the road. A motorist in the center lane honked and swerved around them. As the Olds cleared the open door of the car on the shoulder, Ray looked into the wide eyes of a buxom black woman in purple.

~~~

The vacuum of the big car as it swerved to avoid hitting Grace sucked her hat from her head. She whipped back inside the Honda with a yelp and watched the lovely wide-brimmed Kentucky Derby with white roses and ribbon settle on the Interstate. A second later, a pickup ran over it. One silk rose broke loose and skittered to the shoulder. Grace stared at it, heartbroke. *I loved that church hat.* Her gaze lifted to the big burgundy car backing up to stop a few yards in front of her. She hadn't seen a car like that in decades. A gas hog, Papa would have called it.

Smoke continued to billow from under the hood of sister Arleeta's car. Grace realized she needed to decide, quick, the lesser of two evils: face the possible rage of the gas hog's driver, or stay sitting in a burning vehicle. She grabbed her purse, checked traffic this time, and flung the car door open. As she hustled to put distance between herself and the Honda, braced for it to explode behind her, a gray-haired white man — a long drink of water wearing a t-shirt and blue jeans — climbed out of the other car and walked toward her, his gait stiff-legged, like he'd been sitting too long. That's when she noticed the Ohio license plate.

"You all right, ma'am?" the man called.

A squat boy in a colorful shirt and cargo shorts tumbled out the other side and joined him at the rear of the car.

"Keep the child back!" Grace yelled. "It's on fire!"

The man gave a half-smile and moved

closer. "No, ma'am. That's just radiator steam. Your car's overheated, but it's not gonna catch fire." Her face must have shown her doubt. "I can take a look, if it'll put your mind at ease."

"If you think it's safe."

"Yes, I'm pretty sure it is. My name's Ray, and this is my son — "

"Benjaminraycolton," the boy said, rattling off his name so fast it sounded like one word. Even with his dark sunglasses, Grace recognized the characteristics of Down syndrome in his soft features and the way he shaped his mouth around his tongue. He thrust his small, plump hand out to her. "Hi, honey."

Under normal circumstances, Grace would have chastised a child his age for addressing her in such a brash manner. But these weren't normal circumstances, and she'd been around Roberta and Stanley's little Anna enough to know the boy meant no disrespect. She smiled and took his hand in hers. "Hello, child. My name is Grace."

He gave her a wide smile. "I'm Benny."

Benny's father stepped around them and said, "I'll pop the hood and see what we've got."

Benny let go of her hand and followed his

father. Cars and trucks shot by, oblivious, or indifferent, to the scene on the Interstate's shoulder, filling Grace's senses with grit and exhaust fumes. Tires whined on blacktop, jangling her nerves and crushing the remains of her hat, so much purple straw and shredded ribbon now. *Lord knows what my hair must look like, and after all the time I put into rolling it.* She clutched her purse to her bosom and mouthed a prayer for God's mercy as the man named Ray lifted the hood of Arleeta's car then thrust his arm across his son's chest to hold him back. Grace gasped, but saw no flames. Heard no explosion. Ray spoke to the child and pointed at the engine, as though explaining something. Benny seemed to hang on his father's words. Leaving the hood up, the two turned and walked back to her.

"You've got a busted fan belt," Ray said. "That's why the engine overheated."

"Oh." How could a fan belt make that awful bang? she wondered.

"We can give you a lift to the nearest town. Is there somebody you can call to come get you?"

"I..." Grace didn't know how to answer. Ed. She should call Ed. Of course. That's the logical thing to do. The sane thing. She'd have to explain what happened to his sister's car.

Dear Lord Jesus, what have I done?

The tall stranger stood with one hip cocked, arms loose at his sides, waiting for an answer. His sad eyes set deep in their sockets; exhaustion drew his pale skin taut. He looked like a man who stayed too long at the gaming table and didn't have any more to lose. The defeat in his stance pulled Grace from her own problems. She lifted her chin a notch and said, "Yes, I have family. I'd appreciate that ride, thank you."

"Got anything you want out of the car before we leave?" Ray asked.

"My suitcase."

The boy patted her arm. "I'll get it."

~~~

Too confused by her unexplainable behavior to do anything else, Grace sat in the passenger seat of the classic car and tried to enjoy the ride, the feel of the tires hugging the road, the push of a hot August afternoon against her skin as it lifted and tangled her shoulder-length hair. Sweat prickled her upper lip and ran down the middle of her back.

"Where are you two gentlemen headed?" she asked, determined to carry on a normal conversation.

Benny thrust his head between the bucket seats. "Grand Canyon."

"Sit back, son. Put your seatbelt on."

The boy gave an audible sigh over the rush of heavy air bombarding the interior of the car, but he did as told without argument. Grace appreciated a well-mannered child and the easy way his father spoke to him.

"How 'bout you, ma'am?" Ray asked, turning that low, easy voice her way. "Where you headed?"

Grace felt her precarious hold on normal slip. "I thought I was going to Las Vegas."

"Vacation?"

"Reunion...of sorts." Her answer hit her ears with an unmistakable thud of defeat. "Haven't been there in years."

"It's changed a lot, from what I hear," Ray offered.

Despair twisted at Grace's control. "Yes, I heard that too."

"If you didn't drive your car long after the belt broke, you could be back on the road again before you know it."

"I drove 'til it wouldn't drive no more."

Ray gave a low whistle. "You prob'ly blew the engine."

Sister Leeta's going to have a hissy fit.

"It might be a while before you get to Vegas," Ray said.

Resigned to the fact she'd never see the Stardust again, Grace pasted a smile to her face that felt as fake as a store-bought biscuit and asked, "Is this your first time to the Grand Canyon?"

"It is for my boy. I was there years ago." He shot her a look that startled her with its nakedness. "Seems we're both lookin' for a reunion of sorts."

Grace stared back at him for a long moment before answering. "It would seem so." She snuck a peek at the speedometer. "You're certainly in a hurry to get there."

Benny leaned forward again. "Dad's feet itch."

The edges of Grace's fake smile relaxed. "Amen to that."

~~~

Ray heard his passenger give a distressed "Oh," and looked over at her. The woman had her head bent over her purse while she dug through one of the pockets.

"Something wrong?" he asked.

She turned her purse and dug in the other side. "I can't find..." More digging.

Any other time, Ray would have looked

away and not given it another thought. The contents of a woman's purse baffled him. Virginia used to pull things out of hers that left him speechless. Her survival kit, she called it. But Grace looked on the verge of panic. Or tears. *Crap, don't start crying.* Nothing made him feel more uncomfortable and helpless than a woman's tears. "What'd you lose?" he asked, hoping to calm her by remaining calm himself.

"My keys."

As soon as the words came out her mouth, her pawing stopped and she pulled a ring of keys from her purse. She held them in front of her and stared at them like she'd never seen them before.

Trepidation prickled up Ray's spine. "There ya go," he said around a throat gone dry.

She turned her head and looked at him, her eyes as wide as when he'd nearly run her down. The look scared him more this time. "These are my house keys," she said. As though that explained everything.

The blast of a car horn let Ray know he was drifting into the next lane. He shivered and pulled his attention back to the road. The woman must have a screw loose. Why else would she act so confused over her own house keys? He heard the keys drop into her purse.

An echoing jingle came from behind him. "Here, honey." Benny thrust a ring of keys between the bucket seats.

At first Ray thought his son offered Grace the keys he carried around in his cargo shorts, the ones that didn't go to anything anymore. But a quick glance showed a Honda key dangling from the ring. Benny must have put them in his pocket after he pulled Grace's suitcase from the trunk.

Grace gave a hesitant smile and took the keys. "Thank you, child."

"Welcome."

~~~

Benny sat in the exact middle of the back seat, pleased he could make Grace smile. There wasn't a seatbelt in the middle, so he took an end from each side and put them together. He rested his foot on his knee and stretched his arms out as far as they would go across the back of the seat. From here, he could look cool in his Terminator sunglasses and watch Grace without anybody telling him not to stare.

Her skin reminded him of maple syrup, and her gentle voice made a warm place in his tummy like Mama's hotcakes. But her color halo looked like the sky before a storm. He didn't think it had anything to do with her car being broke. Not much anyway. Something deep in her heart hurt. Something about dusty stars. He didn't know what that meant, but it must be really important to her. He was glad she had Daddy and him to protect her. They would find a way to get her to the place she needed to be. The place that would make her feel good again.

Satisfied with the way things were going so far, Benny decided to enjoy a smoke. He fished the small, narrow box from the side pocket of his cargo shorts, pulled his white cigarette out from among all the other pretty colors, then put the box back. He puckered his lips around the cigarette, careful not to bite into the wax, and sucked in a deep breath from the corner of his mouth. Leaning back in the seat, he tipped his chin up and blew out pretend smoke.

He remembered Savannah, in the movie *Mad Max: Beyond Thunderdome*, telling the children that finding what's lost ain't easy.

Benny thought she might be wrong.

5: Buckle Up

The phone rang once and Grace hung up. *What will I say if Ed answers? How can I explain my behavior when I don't understand it myself? What am I going to do about Arletta's car?* Gasoline fumes from the corner station engulfed the pay phone and made it difficult to breathe. Heat weighted her limbs. She struggled to stay focused. Finding the house keys after believing she had locked them inside shook her. *Is my forgetfulness getting worse?*

Too many questions rattled in her head.

"Were you able to get a hold of anybody?"

Grace jerked at the sound of Ray's voice from behind her. "No." She dropped her hand from the phone's receiver and stared at the moist print it left. "Nobody's home."

Lord Jesus, now she could add lying to her

list of sins. Maybe. Probably. How could she know for sure if she didn't let the phone ring long enough for anybody to pick up?

"You're welcome to ride with us awhile longer, try calling again in the next town."

Hope laced with suspicion shivered through Grace. She turned and looked up at Ray, her brows drawn low. "Why would you do that?"

She followed his gaze to the car parked a few feet away. Benny sat in the back seat, his chin resting on the sill of the open window, and watched them over the sunglasses perched low on his nose. When he saw her look at him, his face broke into an open smile.

"My son says you need help and it's up to me and him to give it."

Grace wondered if the sudden dance across her skin was a warning or a sign from God. "What about you?" she asked. She used to be better at reading people, when it made the difference between winning or folding. But that was a lot of years ago, and all she got now from looking at the man in front of her was bone-deep tired. "I'll lay odds having a crazy ol' woman ride along wasn't part of your plan."

The corner of his mouth ticked, like it wanted to lift in amusement but couldn't quite muster the energy. "Wasn't much of a plan in the first place." He shrugged and glanced over at his son. "Benny sees things in people I don't. I trust his judgment."

"Your child has a compassionate soul."

"It's more than that. Be damned if I can figure it out though." Ray met her gaze. This time his mouth managed a half smile. "He'll let you have the front seat again."

Grace wanted to say yes. The temptation to believe herself fated to meet these two travelers strained against the burden of guilt and responsibility pressing on her shoulders. How would it look, her going with them?

She got no answer, felt like a fool for even considering the notion. "Thank you," she forced the words past the tightness in her throat, "but you don't need to be taking on my troubles along with your own. I'll stay here and keep trying."

"Suit yourself. Benny'll be disappointed." Ray hesitated, as though considering more, then settled for, "Good luck."

She nodded. "Same to you."

Grace watched him walk away and felt hope die.

~~~

It didn't set right with Ray, leaving the woman standing at the pay phone enclosure alone, suitcase at her feet, but he had to respect her decision. He wasn't as convinced as his son that it fell on them to help her. At least they got her off the Interstate and to a phone.

He climbed behind the wheel of the Olds and glanced in the rearview mirror. "She said no. You wanna ride up front?"

Benny huffed. "Dad, she comes with us."

"I can't force her." Ray made to look back at the pay phone, but the afternoon sun through the windshield caught the corner of his eye, blinding him for a second. When his vision adjusted and he could make out the enclosure, Grace was already gone.

The passenger-side door flew open and a suitcase squeezed between the seat back and frame, thumping on the floor at Benny's feet. Grace plopped into the bucket seat, her purple skirt with its flowers billowing in after her. "I changed my mind," she said, and heaved the wide door closed. "Drive 'fore it can change again."

Benny patted her shoulder. "Hi, honey."

She gave his hand a squeeze. "Hi, sugar." Her too-large brown eyes met Ray's. "You sure you don't mind?"

Ray glanced in the rearview mirror at the joy on his son's face. "No, ma'am." He shot

Grace a smile and turned the key in the ignition. "Buckle up and hang on."

~~~

From the back seat of the Olds, Benny watched the blur of scenery through his Terminator sunglasses. But instead of green trees and mountains and sunshine, he saw a dark highway leading to Miles Dyson's home, where Dyson is about to make a scientific discovery that will destroy the world. Three people change that — change fate and save the world.

Three people.

Benny shifted his gaze to his dad, strong and invincible, driving them to their fate. Nothing would stop him, just like the Terminator. Then to Grace. She had a mission to complete, but she would need help from the Terminator and the smart boy riding in the back seat. Benny imagined himself as that smart boy, future leader of the resistance to overcome the machines that threatened mankind. He would ride on the back of a big, black motorcycle with the Terminator and save the world.

Benny shook his head. No, that wasn't right. The motorcycle was a different movie. Or was it? Sometimes the stories got mixed up in his head. He didn't like when that happened. It made him feel like a dummy for not being able to keep it straight.

He wasn't smart like the boy in the movie; he was a stupid boy and Mama died.

Benny's heart hurt. He didn't have a movie to show him how to fix it. He tried to lie down but the seatbelt squeezed his stomach. Careful to be quiet so his dad wouldn't hear him do it, Benny took the seatbelt off. Using his hands to pillow his head, he curled up and closed his eyes. The vibration of the tires on the road and the warm air against his skin made him sleepy.

~~~

Plumerville. Atkins. Pottsville. Grace watched as they sped past exit after exit. Ray told her to let him know when she was ready to stop and make that phone call. In the meantime, he was going to drive. He said drive like an obsession. With each passing exit, Grace's conscience jangled at her to come to her senses. Yet each passing exit took her closer to the Stardust. She kept her mouth shut as the doused embers of hope struggled back to life. Walls of green foliage, pine and cottonwood, flashed by at seventy miles an hour. Russellville. Across the smooth turquoise water of Lake Dardanelle. London. Knoxville.

She traveled a route unplanned, in a car from the past, a white man at the wheel and his curious son in the back seat. She couldn't shake the feeling the boy controlled the journey and something greater than their physical selves rode shotgun.

Past the Clarksville exit, Grace heard Benny whimper. She looked at the back seat and saw him twitching and mumbling in his sleep, his sunglasses half off, his eyes darting back and forth behind scrunched lids.

"His mama died two months ago," Ray told her. "He's had nightmares ever since."

Grief settled heavy in Grace's heart. "I'm sorry for your loss." She studied Ray's profile, thought she understood the deep sadness pulling at his shoulders. "Is that why you're on this trip?"

Ray drew in a breath that sounded like it came clear from the soles of his shoes. "I thought maybe getting him away from the house for a while would help."

And what about you? Grace wanted to ask. But didn't need to, she realized, thinking on the way he said that one word – drive.

The boy slapped himself in the face, knocking his sunglasses to the floor. He muttered something she couldn't make out and slapped himself again. And then again. The anger in his attack alarmed Grace. "Should I wake him?"

Ray signaled and pulled the car to the side of the Interstate. "I'll take care of it."

Grace watched as he got into the back seat with his son and held him, gently kept him from slapping his face until he was awake, then took a tissue from a side pocket of the boy's shorts.

"Blow your nose, son."

"'kay, Dad."

The tenderness of the scene, the deep pain of loss that bonded father and son, blurred Grace's vision. They clung to each other as though alone on a sinking raft, their survival precarious at best. They needed a rope, a sheltering bosom to console and heal.

Grace felt that dance across her skin again. It did a soft-shoe break down her arm and took her hand.

Thank you, Lord Jesus, for showing me the way.

6: Dusty Stars

They stopped for early supper about an hour west of the Arkansas-Oklahoma border. Grace hadn't eaten since her steel-cut oats with Ed that morning.

Betty Sue's Kitchen looked like a million other greasy spoons across the country. Dark vinyl-covered paneling, baskets of faded plastic flowers hanging from the entryway, chipped Formica tables, framed posters of nameless snowy mountain ranges and countrysides. Years of fried meals hung in the air and clung to the red-checkered curtains. From a set of speakers mounted in opposing corners, Willie Nelson ruminated about blue eyes cryin' in the rain.

"It ain't pretty," Ray admitted, "but these places have real coffee, not that fancy lattecappu-express stuff."

A waitress shifted their direction, moving like she'd been on her feet all day, uncomfortably tight in her white blouse and black slacks, her fading blonde hair pulled into a frizzed bun and her thin lips pinched. Grace hadn't waited tables in forty years, but she empathized with the look. The woman's gaze bounced off Grace, then Benny, and settled on Ray. "What can I get you folks?"

Ray nodded at Grace to go first.

"I'll have a six-ounce sirloin, medium, with sweet potato tots. And coffee."

"Cream with that?" she asked as she scribbled on her pad.

"No, black."

"And you?" The waitress looked up at Ray.

He glanced at Benny. "Fried chicken?"

"Yeah, Dad."

"We'll have two fried chicken dinners. And coffee, black. Lots of it."

"Would he like anything to drink?" the waitress asked, bobbing her head toward Benny.

"A tall glass of milk," Ray answered.

The waitress collected their menus with a singsong "thank you," and hustled off.

"They do that," Ray said, "won't talk to him."

"We have that in common, your boy and me," Grace replied.

"I noticed."

She met Ray's blue eyes – *blue eyes cryin'* – and allowed he likely would notice more than most because of the child sitting next to him.

Benny pulled an eight-count box of crayons from his shorts pocket and turned his paper placemat over. He dumped the crayons on the table, picked up the white one and stuck it in the corner of his mouth like a cigarette.

"No smoking in the restaurant," Ray told him, matter-of-fact like.

"Sorry." The boy put the crayon back in the box and focused on his drawing.

Grace worked her mouth to keep from laughing.

The waitress came back with their drinks, set them on the table with tired efficiency, and left again.

Ray took a sip of his coffee. "Man, that's good." He took another loud slurp, then asked, "So what's your story, Grace?"

She glanced at him over the rim of her cup, took a sip. He got it right about the coffee being good. "My story?"

"You know why Benny and me are on the road. What's so urgent about getting to Vegas that you'd leave your car sitting on the Interstate and hitch a ride with a couple of strange dudes like us?"

"Dusty stars," Benny said without looking up from the yellow house taking shape on his placemat.

Grace stared at the top of his head, surprised, yet not. She set her coffee on the table, careful to control the tremble in her hands. "The Stardust," she corrected. "It's a casino on the Strip. They're tearing it down Thursday."

"And you want to see it before that happens," Ray guessed.

"Yes."

"Mind me asking why?"

Again Benny answered before she could fit two words together. "Her papa."

Grace's eyes slid from the boy to his father. Ray shrugged. "Like I said, he sees things."

Grandma James would have called him a thought reader, Grace mused.

The waitress whisked a new placemat in front of Benny while he pushed his drawing aside and shoved his crayons back into the box. "Thank you, honey," he said, startling a smile from her pinched mouth.

"You're welcome, sweetie." She set their

plates in front of them and asked, "Is there anything else I can get you folks?"

Ray lifted his near-empty cup. "Keep it comin', please."

"Sure thing."

Grace folded her hands in her lap and bowed her head. *Dear Lord, bless this food and those who are about to receive it. May it give us strength on our journey. Amen.*

"Amen," Benny echoed.

Grace lifted her head and looked at the child. He smiled.

Fresh coffee arrived while they ate. Father and son tackled deep-fried chicken next to mounds of mashed potatoes and steamed vegetables. Grace's steak was done perfect, juicy and pink in the middle, and the tots satisfied, though the cook stubbed his toe salting the gravy. When she reached her stomach's limit, she pushed her plate away and said, "Mercy, that hit the spot."

"Way I see it," Ray explained, pushing his own plate aside, "little places like this don't have a lot of money, so they spend it on good food instead of new curtains and paint." He regarded her as he brought his coffee cup up to his mouth. "What's that saying? You can't judge a book by its cover?"

Grace acknowledged the hint. She glanced at Benny still working his way through his mashed potatoes, the fried chicken reduced to a pile of stripped bones on a napkin beside his plate. "Papa was a gamblin' man," she said, her gaze moving to Ray's for his reaction.

~~~

Benny listened to Dad and Grace talk while he finished his potatoes. The chicken was okay, but not as good as Mama's. It reminded him of her anyway, and that made him content.

"Poker was his game," Grace said. "Didn't matter what kind. Long as it was a cash game, he'd play whatever his opponents liked least."

Benny heard Grace's voice change when she talked about her papa. She sounded brighter, like remembering made her content. He liked that word – content. Happy with sad around the edges. Mama used it a lot.

"Papa played all over," Grace continued. "Chicago, San Francisco, St. Louis – any smoke-filled parlor or saloon or basement that had a game going. The Vegas Strip was off-limits, but on the Westside places like the Harlem Club and Brown Derby catered to black folks."

Grace stopped to take a drink of her coffee. Benny gulped his milk and handed his dishes to Dad. Then he pulled out his crayons to finish his picture.

"It ate at Papa," Grace said. "Like a lone star tick burrowing deep under his skin. Casinos on the Strip invited 'Come one, come all,' but Jim Crow guarded the doors. The likes of Sammy Davis, Jr. and Lena Horne could perform on their stages, but when the entertainin' was over, they were showed the back way."

"Why?" Benny asked.

"Prejudice," Dad answered.

That was another word Benny knew. When people treated you different because you weren't like them. He looked at Grace's kind face and beautiful maple syrup skin and couldn't imagine why anybody would prejudice her.

"In 1960, equal rights forced them to change their ways," Grace said. "Papa made a big deal of taking me through the front doors of the Stardust for the first time. Oh my, you should've seen him in his avocado linen suit with mother-of-pearl buttons, struttin' his stuff. He'd waited a long time to – "

She stopped talking and Benny glanced up to see her looking at him. He knew from the unhappiness on her face she almost said something she didn't think he should hear.

"It must have meant a lot to you too," Dad

said in a soft voice.

Grace's eyes sparkled like she might cry. "I never want to forget it."

And that's when Benny saw what scared her. He saw what made her sad and afraid, what made her take a car that didn't belong to her. He was pretty sure of that now, too. It was so she could get back to her memories. She had trouble remembering things, just like he did sometimes. She was afraid some day she would have trouble remembering her family. Benny knew how awful that would be. He never wanted to forget his mama. Not just because she was his mama and he loved her, but because he was the reason she died. That made it his job to remember her.

Grace wiped her eyes with her napkin – "Goodness, look at me, blubbering like a baby" – and gave him a smile. "What's that you're drawing, child?"

Benny held up his picture so she could see it better and said, "Home."

7: The Offer

His son drew a yellow two-story box-shaped house, not the ranch style they left behind in Beavercreek. Stick figures of a man and boy held hands on green spikes of grass. A third stick figure, wearing a pink dress, a gold halo perched over waves of brown hair, flew across the sky toward a fluffy cloud.

Ray's heart squeezed. He didn't miss it: the empty house. The echoes of Virginia's presence. The guilt. He needed more distance. More miles.

He looked at Grace. She had smoothed her hair away from her face but it still had a frazzled wildness to it that made the look in her eyes all the more unsettling. Ray figured she hadn't told him everything, but it didn't matter. Benny was right. The woman needed help. No point wasting time wondering why he and his son had been nominated.

He cleared his throat and Grace looked over at him. "We'll take you all the way to Vegas," he said, "if you want. Don't know about comin' back."

She hesitated a fraction, then nodded. "I need to make that phone call first."

~~~

The pay phone hung on the wall between the restrooms, down a short hallway off the kitchen. Grace fed coins into the phone's slot, punched the number to home, and let it ring.

"H'lo?"

She didn't recognize the gruff male voice. "Who is this?" she asked.

"Who wants ta know?"

Instead of answering the stranger's question, she said, "I'd like to speak to Edward."

"Ain't nobody here by that name."

The line went dead before Grace could ask what number she'd reached. Perturbed, she dropped more coins in the slot and tried again, taking time to concentrate on each number.

"H'lo?"

She hung up. *Dear Jesus in Heaven, I've forgotten my phone number*. Her hands shook as she dug in her purse for the pocket-size directory she carried with her. She turned to the B's but found no listing for Grace and Edward Brown. Why should there be? Most people didn't have to write down their own number. It was everybody else's they needed help remembering.

Fighting against the panic crawling up her back, Grace decided to call Arleeta. Unwilling to trust her memory, she turned to her directory for the number...and paused. What was Arleeta's last name? Grace stared blindly at the small book in her hand. She flipped the page. Her vision came back into focus and relief weakened her knees. Collins. Arleeta and Harold Collins.

Arleeta answered the phone. "Hello?"

"Praise the Lord," Grace said on a heavy sigh.

"Grace? Is that you? Are you alright?"

"Yes, I – "

"Somebody stole my car!"

Arleeta's tearful indignation reached through the line and plucked at Grace's conscience. "I'm sorry, I – "

True to her nature, Arleeta plunged on without listening. "Sister, where are you? Eddy's 'bout out of his mind with worry."

"Yes, I'm sure he is. I'm sorry about your car.

I – "

"Can you believe it? They stole it right out of the church parking lot. The *church* parking lot. In all my days, I never..."

Grace stifled a sob, helpless against her sister-in-law's steamroller ways. Arleeta's voice droned on like a pesky horsefly in her head. The pay phone swam on the wall and an overwhelming need to sit down before she fell down flushed through her. She finally cut in and said, "Leeta, I can't talk right now. Tell Eddy I'm okay, please? Can you do that?"

"Why don't you tell him your own-self? He's sitting at home by the phone, got half the congregation out looking for you. Sister, you don't sound right. Are you sure you're okay? That busybody Gladys said you lit out of services like you had a urgent date with Mother Nature. Where did you say you are again?"

Arleeta's voice got high and sharp, like needles stabbing Grace's ear. Too many questions rushed at her to sort through. "Please," she said, "just tell Eddy I'm alright?" and hung up before the woman got her second wind.

~~~

Two hours later Ray stopped in Oklahoma

City for gas and snacks, then he and Grace decided to spring for a couple rooms at a Motel 6 west of town after Benny started throwing up. It was either the motel or drive with a puke bucket in back, which neither adult considered an option. Ray tossed what was left of the bag of barbecue-flavored potato chips and kicked himself for not paying closer attention to how much the boy had eaten. Virginia wouldn't have let their son buy the chips in the first place. Especially not the biggest bag on the store shelf.

"Eyes bigger 'n your stomach, huh, son?" Ray rubbed Benny's hot back as the boy hugged the toilet bowl and mumbled between heaves. "Don't try to talk. Just let it out."

Benny's heaves settled around midnight. The boy stripped to his briefs, arranged his belongings in a row on the nightstand, then climbed between the sheets of the double bed. In a matter of minutes, he began snoring softly. Ray lay next to him, on top of the comforter, unwilling to do more than kick his shoes off. Arms folded behind his head, he stared at the shadows cast on the ceiling from the streetlight filtering through a slit in the drapes. The drone of the air conditioner filled the room with ambient noise as it blew cool, stale air across the bed.

Ray thought about how rattled Grace looked when she returned to the table after her phone call. No doubt whoever she talked to didn't take kindly to her traveling west with strangers. She didn't give any details, just asked if there'd be time for her to change out of her Sunday best before they got back on the road. Ray got her suitcase from the car.

Grace came out of the restroom at Betty Sue's another cup of coffee later wearing a pair of those short pants that stop just below the knee, and a loose white blouse with three-quarter sleeves. Virginia used to be partial to blouses with three-quarter sleeves. *They're more comfortable than long sleeves and they hide my ugly elbows*, she'd say. Ray had never considered his wife's elbows ugly – had never considered elbows, period – but knew it would have been a waste of breath to try convincing her otherwise. He had a brief notion to tease Grace about her elbows but decided he didn't know the woman well enough to be joking with her that way.

Hell, he didn't know the woman at all outside of her father being a poker player and how the two of them stood up for their civil rights at the Stardust. He respected the significance of what they did, the courage it must have taken. He never had much use for racism himself, especially when the enemy was shooting at him. Didn't matter what color the brother fighting alongside you was in Vietnam. Everybody bled the same shade of red.

One thing for certain, Grace still missed the man she called Papa. That's what bothered Ray. On the drive into Oklahoma City, she told them her papa had been dead for forty-two years. *Forty-two years.* Would he carry the weight of Virginia's death for that long? Would Benny? Were either of them strong enough? How did Grace do it?

Maybe he'd get the chance to ask her, seeing as how she accepted his offer to take her to Vegas. It felt right having her travel with them, and Vegas wasn't that far out of their way. He knew his decision went beyond the simple act of helping another human being in need. Grace filled an empty space.

~~~

Grace worked the tangles from her hair and kicked off her shoes before her conscience shouted at her to stop and reflect. She sat on the edge of the bed in her darkened motel room, hands clasped in her lap. The air conditioner hummed in the unfilled silence and raised goose bumps on her bare arms as she tried to pray.

Dear Lord...

Where to begin? Should she ask for strength or forgiveness? Did she have a right to either? The thought of her dear husband sitting by the phone, worried out of his mind...

Lord Jesus, forgive me.

She looked at the bedside phone but still couldn't remember her number. She hoped against better judgment that Arleeta gave Ed her message without the usual dramatics.

Half the congregation out looking for her. How could she ever show her face in church again? She could already hear the chins wagging, the stories cooked up over why the preacher's wife ran off without a word.

Oh, Eddy, I'm sorry.

I should turn around and go home, Grace thought, repair the damage I've done best I can, before it gets any worse. But the idea churned bitter in her stomach. Going home meant giving up on the Stardust and a piece of Papa. A piece she already forgot once. She shivered, a soul deep tremble that had nothing to do with the temperature of the room. Emptiness waited with open arms.

Grace lowered her head and prayed. *Dear*

Lord, give me strength.

~~~

The scrappy evergreens along the Interstate west of Oklahoma City did little to liven the flat, brown scenery. Grace wrapped her hair in a scarf so she could have the window open without yanking tangles out later. Somewhere down the line, she needed to pick up a small bottle of olive oil for her split ends. And, Lord have mercy, deodorant.

She made a decision last night in her praying and pacing. After the loss Ray and his son suffered, they needed her. Mayhaps it was her guilty conscience attempting to justify her actions, but she had to believe her path belonged with these boys. She had to believe she worked God's plan by traveling on. God would provide.

The day grew warm as Ray's classic car ate fuel and miles. Just outside Clinton, they passed an exit sign for the Lucky Star Casino. So many more casinos than forty years ago, what with Indian gaming on the reservations, and modern day riverboat casinos on the Mississippi. Papa would have been like a kid in a candy store.

"Do you still play poker?" Ray asked.

Grace watched the sign recede in the side

mirror. "After Papa passed on, I gave it up. You have to keep your head, and I couldn't no more."

"Your luck ran out."

She gave him a quick look. "Weren't about luck. Poker's a game of skill, being able to read your opponent, spot their tell."

"Their tell?"

"Toe tapping. Throat clearing. Toyin' with the chips. Tics that give away what kind of hand a person be holding."

"That really work?"

"More times than not. But if it goes south, you have to accept the losses, no matter how good you played." Life dealt her a hand she couldn't win. "Papa was one loss too many."

"What'd you do?"

"I married a preacher."

"You're shittin' me."

His reaction startled a laugh from her. "Been married forty years."

"Mind if I ask why he isn't on this trip with you?"

Self-reproach pressed its sober hand on her conscience. "I don't mind the askin'," she said. "But the answer's complicated."

Ray gave a nod and was polite enough to let it go. He looked in the rearview mirror. "Son, pass that book of maps forward."

"'kay." Benny thrust a large Rand McNally road atlas between the seats.

Ray handed it to Grace. "Would you mind looking for a route that goes around Texas for me?"

She thumbed through the pages to the map of Oklahoma. "You gentlemen have a problem with Texas?"

"Can't go there," Benny piped in.

Ray shot her a don't-ask look. "It's a long story. If you're having second thoughts about travelin' with us, I'll understand."

Grace sniffed. "I've been through that part of Texas. You ain't missin' much, less you like flat."

"Lady, this born and raised Oregonian has had a butt full of flat."

"Then let's see what the Oklahoma Panhandle has to offer. Once we reach Sayre, look for US-283 north."

"Thanks. I figure it'll take more gas, but we'll still get you to Vegas in time."

"I can help pay for gas," Grace offered, "long as we don't spend any more nights in motels." She didn't get a lick of sleep anyway, and by the droop to Ray's eyelids and the way gravity had a hold of his shoulders, he hadn't slept much either. No point wasting the money. The more she could save for the return home, the better.

"'Appreciate that," Ray said. "We'll get where we're goin' quicker if we drive straight through."

~~~

Benny stared at the crooked fence posts zooming by and pretended not to listen to his dad and Grace talk about finances. Mama told him it wasn't polite to listen in on other people's conversations, but sometimes he couldn't help it. The words and thoughts got into his head anyway. He tried not to hear Grace's secret worry about having enough money to get home. Grace had a lot of worries in her head, some of them jumbled together so tight they didn't make sense. But not having enough money came out clear.

Mama always said Daddy didn't have much of a head for managing money, that's why she had to take care of the bills and shopping. Now that Mama was gone, somebody needed to help Daddy with those things.

At first, Benny didn't know what to do. But now they were in the middle of nowhere – and finding a way around Texas – and that gave him an idea.

8: Simon Says

Ray stepped out of the gas station restroom and stood for a minute to survey his surroundings. He'd never seen so much flat country bunched into one place. The burgundy Olds was the only spot of color in the sunburned landscape. A line from *Thelma & Louise* came to mind. *We're not in the middle of nowhere, but we can see it from here.* Hell, if this didn't qualify as nowhere, he would hate to see what did.

Mid-afternoon heat radiated off metal and asphalt. Ray could almost hear the lazy slide of a steel guitar soundtrack in the background as he climbed into the Olds. Grace sat in the front seat, fanning herself with the straw hat she bought when they stopped for lunch in Shattuck.

"Where's Benny?" he asked, glancing at the empty back seat.

"He patted me on the shoulder and told me not to worry. Then he headed for that market over there." She pointed to a whitewashed Mom and Pop across the dusty narrow road from the station. "Maybe he's gone to get us some cold drinks."

Ray stared at the Mom and Pop. Another scene from *Thelma & Louise* played in slow motion through his head. Another dusty, narrow road in the middle of nowhere. The slide of the steel guitar scraped a warning up his spine. "Were you with him the whole time before that?" he asked.

"No. I had to use the ladies' room."

Ray fought to control his shaking hands as he yanked the keys from the ignition and fumbled for the one that went to the glove box.

"What is it?" Grace asked. "What's wrong?"

"Prob'ly nothing," he muttered, but his gut told him otherwise. He unlocked the glove box and popped it open.

A dark hole gaped where the revolver should have been. Ray thrust his hand into the compartment and pushed receipts and warranties, registration and insurance cards around. A long, silver flashlight fell out onto the floor.

Cold fear flushed through Ray. "Crap."

"What is it?"

He straightened and looked at the building across the road. "I think Benny's robbing the store."

~~~

"Good afternoon, ladies and gentlemen," Benny said, holding the gun out in front of him with both hands, his straw cowboy hat pushed down low on his forehead. "This is a robbery."

A lady screamed and Benny forgot what came next. He played the scene over in his head. Thelma standing in the store. People backing away from her. Oh yeah.

"Nobody lose their head," he said, turning in a circle so everybody could see his gun. "Simon says down on the floor."

The screaming lady put both her hands over her mouth. Her eyes looked like big marbles in her face. A man and his little boy just stared at him like he was an alien or something. Nobody got on the floor.

The fat man behind the counter reached out. "Give me that, son, before you hurt somebody."

Benny shook his head. "Simon says – "

"I can't understand a word you're saying," the fat man told him. "Hand over that paint gun now and stop this nonsense."

Benny felt his face get hot. Tears stung his eyes. "Not a paint gun," he shouted. "Put money in a bag!" The heavy gun started to shake in his hands. "Simon says – "

"Boy, I'm not telling you again," the rude fat man interrupted. "Put the toy gun down and stop disturbing my customers." He started to come around from behind the counter. "Where's your folks? Do they know what you're up to?"

Benny backed away. *Mama doesn't know anything 'cause she's dead. Daddy's in the bathroom. We need gas money. This isn't the way it's supposed to go!*

Frustrated, his eyes filled with tears. He didn't know what to do. The fat man got closer. *Run!* He turned, stumbled over his feet, and pounded out the door.

"Wait!" he heard the man yell. "I want to speak to your folks!"

"No!" Benny sobbed.

He didn't want Daddy to see him crying like a baby. He ran around the corner of the store. *Stupid boy!* He hit himself in the forehead with the gun handle. It hurt and made him cry harder. He tried to squeeze behind a row of garbage cans to hide, but the space was too small and one of the cans fell over. The lid popped off with a loud rattle and stuff spilled out.

"Oh man." He had to fix it before anybody saw. Grabbing the edge of the can, he gave a mighty grunt and pulled it upright. Two bags stayed on the ground. The white one squished and smelled bad. Benny thought he might barf before he got it back into the can. The second bag looked like the kind people took to the gym, green and blue, with a zipper and handles. *Why did somebody throw this away?*

It had something in it.

Benny squatted, laid the gun on the ground and unzipped the bag. He looked inside and his heart jumped. Money? Lots and lots of it! He started to pull some out to get a closer look, to make sure it wasn't play money.

"Hey, boy! What're you doing there?"

The fat man had come out a side door near the back of the store. Benny grabbed the gun and the bag and ran.

~~~

Ray saw Benny charge from behind the store, a gym bag in one hand, the Smith & Wesson flashing in the other. Head back, squat legs pumping, his son plowed toward the car, shouting, "Drive, Dad! Go!"

"What's gotten into that child?" Grace asked. "What's that in his hand?"

Before Ray could answer, the bag landed in Grace's lap and Benny launched himself at the open window. He got as far as his belly.

"Go," he grunted, attempting to wiggle the rest of the way through the window and into the back of the car. He tossed the gun on the rear seat and pushed with both hands, but he stuck fast in the window's taper.

Ray had the crazy urge to make a wisecrack about too much fried chicken. Then he looked beyond his son to the big man waving his hand while doing a fast waddle toward them, and the gravity of the situation hit his adrenaline switch.

"Get him in the car and buckle up," Ray ordered. He jabbed the key in the ignition and gunned 360 horses to life.

The big man waddled faster. "Wait! I want a word with you!"

"*Now*, Grace!"

Grace turned in her seat, grabbed Benny by the pants and hauled his butt and legs inside. The boy sprawled on the rear seat with a grunt and Ray threw the Olds in gear. Grace barely got turned around in time to keep from being propelled into the back with Benny as the Olds shot forward.

"Lord have mercy!" she screamed, fumbling for her seatbelt.

The rear tires squalled and left a cloud of burnt rubber in their wake. Ray checked the rearview mirror and saw the big man stop and fan the air, then bend over and brace his hands on his knees.

"Will somebody please tell me what's going on?" Grace shouted. "Where'd that gun come from?"

"Benny's robbed the store," Ray said and mashed the throttle to the floor. The W-30 custom V8 flew up the highway at 110 miles per hour.

"You're not making any sense. Why would the child rob a store?" Grace clutched the edges of her seat. "For heaven's sake, slow down!"

"Slow down?" Ray barked a harsh laugh. "My son just robbed a store and you want me to slow down?"

"No, Dad."

Ray looked at Benny in the rearview mirror. The boy's straw cowboy hat rested low on his forehead and he sat back with that smile of satisfaction he always got when he accomplished something nobody expected him capable of doing.

He robbed the store for sure. "Open the bag, Grace."

She picked it up off the floor and unzipped it. "Oh." She lifted out a neat, green bundle of twenties. "Oh, my."

"Don't wave it around for the whole world to see." Ray fixed his gaze on the highway and muttered, "My son robbed a store." He couldn't stop saying it, couldn't stop hearing Louise's voice in his head like a skip in the movie track. *You robbed a goddamn store? Thelma...*

"No, Dad." Benny leaned forward. "I *found* the money. In the garbage."

"Don't lie to me, son. I've seen the movie almost as many times as you. And give me that gun."

"Da-a-ad."

"I said give me the damned gun!"

Benny started crying.

"Don't swear at the child," Grace said.

"That *child* just committed armed robbery!"

"We'll go back. Return the money. Explain to the store manager that it was all a mistake. The boy didn't know what he was doing. Given his disability – "

"No!" Ray shook his head to shut her up. He hated people talking about Benny's Down syndrome like it was a handicap, especially in the boy's earshot, and especially as an excuse for bad behavior. Virginia made excuses for their son. *I just don't know what to do with Benny. I expect too much from him. He'll always be a child.* She'd babied him. That always rankled Ray.

"No," he told Grace, quieter this time but with no less insistence. "Benny knew what he was doing. It's my fault for not keeping a closer eye on him. It's my fault for letting him get his hands on a loaded gun."

Exactly why Virginia hadn't wanted it in the house.

He looked hard at Grace and lowered his voice even further to make sure Benny couldn't hear. "That handgun is unregistered and I've taken it across I don't know how many state lines. I'm the one they'll arrest, and then what happens to my boy?"

The change in her eyes told him she understood. Benny thrust the gun past her face and she yelped.

Ray reached over his shoulder and took the gun by its barrel. "Put your seatbelt on, son."

"'kay."

"Grace, take the wheel."

She did without question. Ray opened the revolver's cylinder and ejected the rounds. *No empty casings. Thank God.* He put the rounds in the breast pocket of his t-shirt and snapped the cylinder into place. Then he took the steering wheel from Grace and handed her the gun.

"Put that away," he said. "We're gettin' the hell outta Dodge while I think about what to do next."

~~~

Grace felt better knowing the handgun was unloaded as she placed it back in the glove box. She never had much use for guns. Papa carried a .38 derringer in his vest pocket and insisted she know how to fire it. She was ten at the time. Mother sucked her teeth in disapproval, which was all the incentive Grace needed to give it a try. Papa set an empty Orange Crush bottle on a rotted fence post somewhere outside of Chicago and Grace shattered it with her first shot. Deadeye, Papa called her. The recoil about jerked the small pistol from her grip and her hand shook uncontrollably as she gave it back to him. She never wanted to shoot it again. Papa didn't push the issue.

She sold the derringer after Papa started getting bad off enough that she feared he'd try to use it on himself.

The big car ate a couple more minutes worth

of two-lane before Grace chanced another look in the bag. Stack after stack of bundled twenty-dollar bills. *The Lord shall provide* went through her thoughts but she quickly hushed the notion. "What's a small market out here in the middle of nothin' doing with this kind of money?" she wondered aloud.

"What're you saying?" Ray asked.

"Maybe the child's telling the truth. Maybe he *did* find the bag."

Grace could see Ray chewing on the idea, his eyes no longer focused on the road but turned inward on his thoughts. Finally he admitted, "Benny's never been able to lie worth a damn." He looked in the rearview mirror. "Where'd you say you got this bag?"

"Garbage can," Benny sulked.

Ray shook his head. "That don't make sense."

"I did!" Benny's voice hitched on a sob.

Grace's heart went out to the boy. His father, his best friend and hero, didn't believe him. "Suppose somebody put the bag there by mistake," she offered.

"It'd take a real idiot to *accidentally* throw out – " Ray cast her a sidelong glance. "How much money are we talking about?"

"Looks close to a hundred thousand."

He whistled.

Grace continued her conjecturing. "Could be drug money. Maybe Benny interrupted a switch, a payoff, a whatever-you-call-it." She looked around at the no-man's land of scrub brush and horizon speeding by. "But why out here?"

"Well hell, how should I know?"

"Either way, we should put it back, in case whoever it belongs to – "

"No!" Benny cried. "Finders keepers!"

"There's still the little matter of the gun," Ray reminded her. "I doubt that clerk appreciated having it waved in his face. He's probably called the cops by now."

"How can you be sure he even saw the gun?"

"I know my son." Again Ray looked in the rearview mirror. "Did you try to rob the store like Thelma?"

"Yeah, Dad."

"Did you hold the gun out where everybody could see it and tell them 'Simon says,' like Thelma?"

"Yeah."

Grace frowned. "Who's Thelma?"

"*Thelma & Louise*? You know, the movie?"

"Yes, I know the movie." A feeling of

unreality came over her as everything began to settle into place. "*That's* why we're not going through Texas?"

"Yep."

She remembered only snatches of the story. Her youngest daughter, Olivia, had insisted she watch the movie with her. Grace found it a little too farfetched for her liking. The ending, though – the women holding hands as they plunged into the Grand Canyon – was entertainment legend. She studied Ray's determined profile and wondered just how deep his grief went. She remembered the times Papa railed because he couldn't find his derringer. When Grace asked him what he wanted it for, he shaped his fingers into a pistol and pointed at his temple.

Was Ray suicidal?

Grace swallowed the wad of cotton in her throat and slanted him a look from the corner of her eye. She carefully asked, "What do you boys plan to do when you get to the Grand Canyon?"

Her voice must have given her away, because Ray looked at her like she'd gone mad. "Good God, woman. We're not plannin' to drive off the edge."

Benny thrust his face between the bucket

seats, his red, puffy eyes a contradiction to his huge grin. "We're gonna fly."

9: Methane

Ray could tell from Grace's silent, wide-eyed stare that Benny's declaration unsettled her. Hell, it unsettled him a mite, too. Did his son really believe Louise's car sprouted wings at the end of the movie? That the women somehow lived happily ever after? Is that why he wanted to go to the Grand Canyon?

The right front tire of the Olds drifted onto the loose shoulder and Ray jerked the steering wheel and his thoughts back into line. He had more important things to worry about right now. Like what to do with the bag of money in Grace's lap. And who it belonged to. And were the police after them? He couldn't risk arrest and what seeing him hauled off to jail would do to Benny. Not when the boy had already lost his mama. The authorities would most likely put Benny in Karen's custody, if it came to that. But Ray couldn't rule out crazy Aunt Georgia. He couldn't allow his son to end up with that woman. Gin would never forgive him.

Like in *Thelma & Louise*, their road trip had taken a wild-ass detour. He needed to fix things before they got any worse. Just how, he didn't know.

One thing he did know for certain. He looked at Grace and said, "It's time we let you out."

"No, Dad!"

"Don't interrupt, son. This is between me and Grace."

"But – "

"I mean it."

Ray heard Benny huff, glanced in the rearview mirror and saw the boy plop back in his seat and start talking to himself, gesturing as though trying to explain his point to an unresponsive audience. Some time ago, Ray asked him who he talked to when he did that and Benny said simply, "Me." "Do you get an answer?" Ray asked, only half teasing. He really did want to know if his son had the ability to carry on two-sided conversations in his head. Benny looked at him like he couldn't believe his own dad would ask such a stupid thing. Finally he sighed and said, "Yeah."

Now, driving hell-bent-for-election into God-only-knew-what, Ray turned his attention back to Grace and said, "I'm serious. No need for you to get mixed up in this mess."

~~~

A jolt went through Grace so strong and sudden she jerked as if from an electrical shock. The hairs on the back of her neck buzzed. She reached her hand to the spot and felt the buzz through her fingertips.

"You okay?" Ray asked.

Grace turned and looked at Benny. He had taken his sunglasses off, and when her eyes met his, he gave her a knowing grin. Like a megaphone in her head, she heard him fluent and clear, clearer than if he tried to speak the words out loud. *You have to see your papa at the Stardust.*

Lord have mercy, the boy ain't just a thought reader. He's a telegrapher. A strong one. Grace wondered if the child knew his full abilities. Once again she suspected something beyond their understanding controlled this journey and Benjamin Ray Colton be their agent.

She faced forward and told Ray, "I expect

you to honor that offer of a ride."

His hands worked the steering wheel like wringing wet laundry. He stared at the road, his jaw tight. "That offer was made before my son pulled a loaded weapon on innocent people."

"All the more reason you need me."

His hands stopped their wringing. The look he shot her said it all. The man was scared. She saw that look on her papa's face but once. Then as now, she knew she had two choices: fall to her knees and take what come, or step up and do what needed doing. Mayhaps it be a fault of hers, but she never had been one to crawl.

"You got any suggestions?" Ray asked, his voice downright painful.

Grace tossed a glance at the speedometer. "If you don't want to attract attention, you might ease up on that lead foot."

~~~

Benny understood why his dad got upset over him trying to rob the store. Louise got upset with Thelma too. But the money he found didn't come from the store. He didn't steal it. He wished Daddy could be happy about that. Now they had enough to take Grace to Las Vegas and go to the Grand Canyon. They wouldn't have to worry about the cost of gas or motel rooms, and they could eat as much as they wanted to.

But not barbecued potato chips. He didn't want to ever see another bag of those, *ever!*

He felt bad they had to pay for a motel room so he could be sick in the toilet. Motel rooms cost a lot, just like gas and food. But that wasn't a problem anymore. He took care of it, just like Thelma did after that lying cowboy stole their envelope of money. He didn't know who put the bag in the garbage; it didn't matter. Finders keepers.

Benny dug a tissue from his cargo pocket and blew his nose. There was only one tissue left in the plastic wrapper. If he didn't stop crying like a baby, he'd have to buy more at the next store. He wouldn't have to use any of the bag money either. He still had some of his allowance. Mama taught him how to save and buy only things he really needed.

He finished wiping his nose and pulled the tissue away. "Gah!" The awfullest smell he ever smelled sucked up his nose and into his mouth. It grabbed the back of his throat and he gagged. For a scary second, he thought he would start throwing up again. He slapped his hands over his face, but the smell leaked through. Smells like somebody bombed the outhouse, as Daddy liked to say after a fart.

Benny shot an accusing look at the back of his dad's head. "You're sick!" he said, his words muffled because he didn't want to uncover his mouth and nose. "Go to the hospital!"

"Mercy." Grace yanked her hat off and fanned her face.

Daddy looked at both of them, his eyes scrunched like he was trying hard not to crack up. "I didn't do it."

Benny looked at Grace.

"That stink ain't me!" she squeaked.

Daddy's eyes watered. "Damn! Must be a pig farm around here somewheres."

A scene from *Mad Max: Beyond Thunderdome* popped into Benny's head. *Where Bartertown gets its energy. From pig shit cometh...* "Methane," he said out loud.

"Boy, I'll say!" Daddy made a choked sound and put his arm across his mouth and nose and steered the car with one hand.

Grace fanned her hat harder. "Smells like enough methane to run the whole blessed country." Benny thought her hat might fly apart any second. "Forget what I said about slowin' down. Get us outta here!"

Daddy put his other hand back on the steering wheel. "Yes, ma'am!"

Benny felt his body press deep into the seat and a hot gust of stinky air pushed at his cowboy hat as Daddy made the car fly like the wind.

Grace jammed her hat down far on her head and held tight to the bag of money still on her lap. "I'll say one thing. You boys sure know how to show a lady a good time."

~~~

A handful of miles later, the heat and excitement of the day caught up with Ray's passengers. Benny lay stretched out on the back seat, snoring under his cowboy hat. Grace's head bobbed as though supported on a spring. Her hat had joined the road atlas at her feet. Before nodding off, she had stowed the bag of money on the floor behind Ray's seat.

A shit-load of money.

What the hell am I doing?

Grace was right. They should have returned it. If he hadn't reacted like some idiot in a movie scene, there would have been time to toss the bag out and get away. But insomnia, and a pervading anger over Virginia's death, had taken its toll on his ability to react with logic. The farther he drove, the worse his chances got of waltzing into a police station and explaining what happened without

116

looking like a criminal.

What if the money's owner comes looking for it? Would the guy accept a simple apology? Or shoot first and ask questions later? Ray didn't have the answers. He felt as void as the landscape.

And right or wrong, he refused to turn around.

Damn it, Virginia. Why'd you have to go and die on me?

He squinted against the late afternoon sun as he drove into Boise City, Oklahoma. In the center of Main Street stood the Cimarron County Court House, a three-story brick building with white columns, surrounded by manicured lawns. A sign in front showed the road circling the building and four roads branching out from it like compass points. Ray didn't see US-412 mentioned. He drove around to the back of the courthouse and picked up Main Street again. With his navigator asleep and the atlas out of reach, he figured to just continue heading west.

The air had cleared of hog farm stench. Low shrub-covered buttes and plateaus broke up the monotonous scenery. Ray rolled his head to work the kinks out of his neck and kept driving. He intended to stay on US-412 to cross into New Mexico, then pick up I-25. But when he stopped for gas at a place called the Kenton Merc – a small, false-front building with a wagon wheel bench out front, a Coke machine at one end and two gas pumps at the other – Grace sputtered awake, picked up the road atlas and informed him they were too far north, close to the Colorado border on 325.

"Black Mesa," she said, "elevation 4,973 feet, highest point in Oklahoma."

Ray rubbed at the grit in his eyes and pulled in a long, slow breath. "Does it hook up with Interstate 25 anywheres?"

She turned to a new page, studied it a few seconds. "Eventually."

"That's good enough for me." In the rearview mirror, he saw Benny sit up, right his cowboy hat and look around. "Nice nap, son?"

"Yeah." The boy yawned and patted his belly. "I'm hungry."

Ray glanced over at the neon open sign in the shape of an ice cream cone taking up a window of the Merc. "Let's go see what we can find."

10: Bossie, Bossie

A short while after leaving Kenton, they crossed the border and Oklahoma 325 became New Mexico 456. "The Dry Cimarron Highway," Grace read from the atlas. She looked up at the rough two-lane heading straight into a sun hung low on the horizon. Layered flat-top mesas cast long shadows over the land. The warm evening air smelled of dried grasses and cow pies, reminding her of Grandma and Grandpa James's farm. An occasional dirt road cut off through the barbed wire fence – to seemingly nowhere at times, to a glint of light in the distance at others. "It would take hardy stock to live out here," she commented, remembering how Grandpa James used to get up before daylight and didn't stop until long after dark.

"You'd have to like cows a whole bunch," Ray remarked.

Benny called from the back seat, "Here, Bossie, Bossie."

Grace chuckled. "Sounds like you've had yourself some experience."

Ray shot her a wry smile. "More like too many *Bonanza* reruns."

~~~

The last of the day's light faded with the pavement. Gravel crunched under the car's tires. Ray slowed and asked, "You sure this goes through?"

Grace shrugged in apparent unconcern. "The little gray line on the map says it does."

"Alright then."

"We lost, Dad?"

"Nope. I know right where we are."

Grace snorted and Ray did the same, glad for her company. The rhythmic sound of crunching gravel, punctuated by an occasional *ping* from a rock bouncing off the undercarriage, eased the tension between his shoulders. He concentrated on the stretch of road caught in the headlights, kept his speed down enough to give himself time to see potholes or washboards, but fast enough to stay ahead of the dust trail following them. He welcomed the opportunity to occupy his thoughts on driving and nothing else.

The car rumbled over a cattle guard and Benny poked his head between the seats. "What was that?"

"Ranchers put metal grills across the road to keep their cattle from getting out," Ray explained. "Sit back. Everything's fine."

Two seconds later Ray had to eat his words when he heard a disheartening *Pffft!* and the Olds slued to the left. "Crap." He muscled the car to the side of the road and shut off the engine. Fine dust rolled in through the open windows.

"Flat tire?" Grace asked.

"Would seem so."

"Oh, man," Benny groaned, plopping back in the seat.

Ray reached over and got the flashlight out of the glove box. "This shouldn't take long," he said to Grace, then lowered his voice and added, "I know it's unloaded, but keep an eye on that for me, please?"

She glanced at the gun and nodded.

The spare tire was in the trunk, buried under the camping equipment. Benny tagged along and helped Ray move things out of the way.

"Use this?" his son asked, holding up the battery-operated lantern.

"Good idea, son."

~~~

Benny grinned. He liked having good ideas. Daddy took the lantern and gave him the flashlight to hold onto. "You get the jack," his dad told him. "I'll get the tire iron and the spare."

"'kay." He had helped his dad change a tire before, so he knew what the jack looked like. Dad kicked a block of wood under the back tire, then they took the rest of the stuff to the front of the car.

"Musta found a sharp rock," Daddy said when he saw the flat tire. He put the jack under the bumper and stuck the handle in. "Pump on that 'til I say to stop."

Benny gave his best Hulk roar as he pushed down hard on the handle and the car started to raised up. Before it got very high, Dad told him to take a break so he could loosen the lug nuts. Then Benny pumped on the handle some more, until the car was high enough to take the flat tire off.

While he waited for his dad to put the spare on, Benny watched bugs fly around in the light from the lantern. He could hear more bugs making chirping noises in the dark. The night air made his shirt flap a little and felt good on his sticky skin. "Dad?"

"What, son?"

"I gotta pee."

"Take the flashlight and go find a bush to water."

Benny didn't like the dark very much. He shined the flashlight from side to side, making sure nobody could jump out and scare him. He walked in front of the car for a long ways, until he was sure Grace couldn't see him in the light from the lantern. He found a bush that wasn't very far off the road, next to a fence, and made his way over to it. The dry grass crunched under his shoes and the tiny bugs jumped up and tickled his legs. He laid the flashlight on the ground so it shined on the bush, unzipped his fly and started watering.

He almost finished his business when he heard a noise. It sounded like footsteps behind the bush. Something big. Benny shook off and hurried to get tucked in and zipped, but the zipper stuck. He yanked and yanked on the pull thing, but it wouldn't move.

The footsteps came closer. Benny forgot about his stuck zipper, picked up the flashlight and shined it at the sound. Two giant, glowing eyes stared back at him and he screamed.

~~~

Ray stood at the back of the car, stowing the flat tire in the trunk, when Benny's scream injected hot ice through his chest. He looked up as the flashlight went out. Grabbing the tire iron and lantern, he ran around the side of the car, made it to the driver's door at the same time Grace turned on the headlights. Benny sat spotlighted at the side of the road, his shoulders hitching with sobs. A cow hung her head over the fence, watching the goings-on.

"Need help?" Grace asked through the open window.

Ray laid the tire iron down, said, "I got it, thanks," and walked over to his son. His knees popped as he squatted next to the boy and saw the flashlight clutched in his hand, the end missing and the batteries scattered. "Guess Bossie heard ya callin' her, huh?"

"Yeah."

"Stop crying now. That cow ain't gonna hurt you."

Benny held up the flashlight. "I broke it," he sobbed.

Ray realized the boy's tears had nothing to do with the cow. He knew how his son felt about breaking things, how it tore him up inside. Especially if it was something that couldn't be fixed, like a shattered Dresden vase. "Let's see if we can find the end cap and the batteries," he said.

Benny sniffed and wiped at his eyes with the backs of his hands. "'kay."

The pieces hadn't gone far. Ray showed his son how to put the flashlight back together, then turned it on. "Good as new," he said, and Benny smiled. Ray helped him to his feet. "Close your barn door, son."

~~~

Grace gazed out the open window at the stars, her hat in her lap. The warm night air tugged at her hair. She hadn't seen stars this big since...well, she couldn't remember. And for once, not remembering didn't bother her. She gave a small humph of surprise.

"What?" Ray asked, his voice a whisper. Benny slept in the back.

Grace shrugged. "Somehow things don't seem as important out here." She looked over at him, his features cast in eerie shadows from the dash lights. Exhaustion pulled at him, but the day's tension appeared gone. He had his left elbow resting out his window, his right wrist draped over the steering wheel, like the car drove itself and the steering wheel was just a place to park his hand. He didn't say anything to her comment, but she could see him mull it over then give a slow nod. It didn't seem possible she met him only a day and a half ago, what with the afternoon they had.

"You got any kids, Grace?"

"Four. Luella and her husband own a bakery in Cincinnati. Eddy Junior's a dentist in North Little Rock. Olivia's a preschool teacher, and Sidney, our youngest boy, is doing missionary work in Guatemala."

"Grandkids?"

"Six, and our first great-grandbaby's on the way." Sibyl and her husband, Isaac, made the announcement last month. "Is Benjamin an only child?"

"No, my daughter, Karen, and her husband live a couple blocks from our place in Beavercreek. They've got twin boys, two years old."

"Lord have mercy, I bet they're a handful."

"That they are. But Karen's a good mother, had a lot of practice on her little brother. She didn't want us to make this trip, for fear something might happen." Ray sighed. "Guess she was right."

"Why do you suppose he did it?" Grace asked.

"I figure he heard us talking about the cost of things and got worried. He's always been a worrier. If something's not right, he sets out to fix it." He told her about his wife's vase and how Benny cut himself trying to put it back together. "One time, when he was about two and still in diapers, he was playing on the kitchen floor while Virginia washed dishes, and this turd fell out of his diaper. Well, he knew that wasn't good and he had to do something about it. So he picks up the turd and chucks it into the dishwater."

"Oh!" Grace slapped her hand over her mouth to keep from waking Benny.

Ray flashed her a smile. "Gin didn't know whether to laugh or cry. She finally fished the turd out of the dishwater and showed Benny that it belonged in the toilet and how to flush after." He paused and cocked his head. "Huh."

"What is it?"

"Benny used the toilet from then on to do his number two."

Grace smiled. "Hold onto those memories just as hard as you can."

He nodded. "In the end, that's all ya got left."

His words sent a cold wind through her. She squeezed her eyes closed and bit her upper lip, willing her panic into submission. *I am weak but Thou art strong*...

"You okay?"

She opened her eyes to find Ray looking at her. "I...forget things," she told him, her voice shakier than she cared for. "Sometimes I can remember a thing from forty years back like it happened yesterday. Sometimes not. Sometimes five minutes ago..."

He gave a knowing nod and she didn't bother to finish. Instead, she said, "Papa died from it."

"I'm sorry, Grace."

He meant it, too. She heard it in his voice, saw it in the shift of his hand from being draped over the steering wheel to gripping it. Grace was glad to have it off her chest. She looked up at the stars again, felt the night air's caress on her skin. "They say doin' new things keeps the brain healthy," she commented, her tone intentionally over-bright.

Ray busted out with a laugh that woke Benny.

11: Bad Man

Benny ate his oatmeal, peaches, and toast even though he really wanted fried chicken. Daddy said no, the restaurant didn't serve dinner for breakfast. Oatmeal will keep you regular, Daddy told him. Mama used to say keeping regular was important, so Benny didn't argue. Grace ordered oatmeal too. She thanked God for hers, but Benny didn't think it tasted good enough to be thankful for.

From his booth seat next to the window, he watched a freight train go by on the tracks across the street. The sun coming up on the other side flashed between the cars. *Clack, clack, flash. Clack, clack, flash.* Daddy and Grace looked tired because they stayed up all night driving and talking. Benny tried to stay awake, but the rumble of the car made him fall asleep.

He dreamed about hiding from the police and a cow breathing on his head.

He lifted another spoonful of oatmeal to his mouth as a shiny red car parked beside Daddy's Olds. *Clack, clack, flash.* A skinny little man got out. Benny shivered and put his spoon back in the bowl. The man's yellow hair stuck up like it hadn't been combed in a long time, and he must have got his black and white striped shirt out of a dirty-clothes basket, because it was all wrinkled. A cigarette hung from his mouth and he squinted when the smoke got in his eye.

The man's halo, the color of a blister with the skin picked off, scared Benny. The man was mad. Really mad. He looked into the back of Daddy's car, saw the bag of money on the floor – Benny knew that's what he was looking for – and grabbed the door handle. But Daddy remembered to lock the doors. The mad man got madder when it wouldn't open. *Clack, clack, flash.* He went around to the door on the other side and yanked on the handle lots of times. It wouldn't open either. Benny thought he gave up because he went back to his own car then. But instead of getting in, he opened the trunk and pulled out a long, shiny piece of metal. *Clack, clack.* The train ended and the sun shined full in Benny's eyes. The man's head snapped up and he looked straight at the restaurant window.

Startled, Benny jumped sideways on the bench and bumped into Daddy, making the scrambled eggs fall off his fork.

"Whoa, son, what's wrong?"

Benny pointed out the window. "Bad man."

~~~

At first Ray thought his son said Batman. But that thought lasted all of two seconds when he followed Benny's finger and saw the greasy little weasel trying to get into the Olds. The asshole had a slim jim shoved between the glass and rubber of the driver's side window, fishing for the lock linkage.

~~~

Grace heard Batman too. She looked out and saw the rumpled, blond-headed man, thirtyish, trying to get into Ray's car an instant before Ray exploded from the booth and pounded for the door. "Stay put," he ordered, and banged the door open so hard it rattled a display of travel brochures on the wall.

"Oh Lord." Several things raced through Grace's mind at once. The gun in the glove box. The bag of money on the floor. The look of rage in Ray's eyes.

"Don't worry, dear," a dough-faced woman in the next booth shouted. She had a cell phone pressed to her ear and a take-charge set to her beefy jaw. "I'm calling 9-1-1."

The police.

Sick dread bloomed in Grace's stomach. She fished a couple bills from her wallet and laid them on the table. Sliding from the booth, she reached for Benny's hand. "Come on, sugar, we gotta go."

Benny took her hand without argument. By the time they reached the parking lot, the wannabe car thief lay flat on his back on the concrete, out cold, a spot of blood growing on his lower lip. His bent cigarette smoldered a few feet from his head. Ray stood over him, massaging his right fist.

"Get in the car, Ray," Grace ordered and pointed Benny to the passenger's side.

Ray didn't seem to hear her, just stared at his victim as though willing the man to get up so he could knock him down again.

"Now!" Grace grabbed his arm and made him look at her. "The police are comin'."

~~~

They left Springer and headed south on I-25.

"Damn car thief," Ray said. "A man pays hard-earned money for a new vehicle, keeps it in vintage condition, and along comes some asshole thinking he can just help himself."

Guilt tugged at Grace thinking about Arleeta's car abandoned on the Interstate back in Arkansas. Vintage? No. Stolen? Close enough. How would Ray react to knowing he harbored a car thief? John the Apostle said the truth shall set you free, but Grace decided the truth could wait awhile. She checked the mirror on her side every few seconds, expecting to see flashing red and blue lights behind them.

A thought kept tickling at the back of her mind. She even reached up and scratched at it. Ray went on and on about how his car had become a collector's item and worth more than he paid for it brand new in '69 and no snot-nosed weasel was going to get his hands on it. All the while Grace felt that tickle.

They put maybe five miles between them and the restaurant, before the tickle bloomed into something she could identify. She turned and looked at Benny. He sat back with his hands cupped behind his head, cowboy hat tipped low, a look of utter satisfaction on his face.

"Why you little stinker," Grace said. He looked surprised for a second, then grinned at her. "You knew all along, didn't you?"

Ray shot her a questioning frown. "Knew what?"

"That man weren't after your car." Grace cocked her head toward the back seat.

Ray's gaze shifted to the rearview mirror. "Aw hell."

~~~

Benny never had somebody be able to hear his thoughts without him trying before. His happiness about Daddy punching the bad man and keeping the bag of money safe must have gotten bigger than his brain could hold and some leaked out. He was happy that Grace heard him.

Daddy's color halo had a stormy sky look to it, like his feelings were all mixed up and ready to explode. If he could get some sleep, Benny thought, maybe he could be happy too. Mama always said a good night's rest made things look better in the morning.

Daddy shook his head. "I know we agreed no more motels, but I gotta stop. I'm 'bout dead on my feet and my hand hurts like hell."

Grace opened the book of maps. "Santa Fe's coming up. We can find a motel there, ice your hand, lay low for a while. It's easier to hide in a large city."

Daddy gave her that look he got when something surprised him – one eyebrow up, one eyebrow down. "Sounds like you've done this before."

I have. Benny heard it in his head, but then Grace shut the thought off.

"I've watched my share of movies," she said out loud.

Adults had a way of telling the truth and a lie at the same time. It confused Benny. He tried it once and got himself into a lot of trouble.

Daddy drove without talking for a few seconds, then said, "If the money really belongs to Mustang man, you can bet he'll find us again." He looked at Grace. "When he does, we'll give him the bag."

Benny's happiness flew away.

~~~

The motel room had cable TV. While his dad slept on top of the bed, Benny sat cross-legged on the floor, using the end of the bed as a backrest, and watched *Pirates of the Caribbean: The Curse of the Black Pearl*. He had it turned down low and could hear Grace snoring in the room next door.

He'd seen the movie before. Lots of times. Captain Jack Sparrow's boat sinks so he has to find another one, but he ends up in jail and the doggie won't give him the key to get out. The Black Pearl sails into port and shoots cannon balls at the town and blows everything up. The pirates want their gold back.

Benny realized it was all about treasure – finding it and keeping it. He found a bag of treasure. Now he had to figure out how to keep it. If he could just get Daddy to parley with him, but Daddy didn't take him serious.

Everybody takes pirates serious. The people of the town ran away screaming. The pirates took what they wanted and did what they wanted.

Benny remembered seeing a neat store across from the motel when he carried his suitcase up the stairs. He told Daddy he wanted to go there but Daddy said it had to wait 'til after he took a nap. Benny twisted around and peeked at his daddy's mouth hanging open and his closed eyes.

Nighty night, Benny thought, and quietly put his shoes on.

12: Pirates Can't Swim

"Ray honey."
"Gin? Is that you?"
"You need to wake up now."
"But I'm so tired."
"You need to look after our son."
"Benny's fine. Gin, I – "
"He can't swim."

Ray's eyes flew open and he launched from the bed. Heart lobbing, he didn't waste time searching the room but went straight to the window and jerked the drapes open.

The motel wrapped around a small swimming pool. In the middle of the pool, a pirate wearing a three-pointed black hat straddled an air mattress and swung a plastic sword at two boys maybe a couple years younger than him. The boys treaded water around the air mattress and took turns lunging and grabbing. Each swing of the sword tipped the pirate drunkenly.

~~~

Benny waved and yelled, "Hi!" when he saw his dad come out of the motel room.

He forgot to hold on, forgot about the game with the boys trying to take his ship. One of the boy's grabbed his leg and pulled him into the water. Benny swung his sword but missed. Water went up his nose and burned. He put his feet down to stand but couldn't feel the bottom. He opened his mouth to yell for help but the water choked him. Too late he remembered Daddy telling him not to breathe under water. He always remembered too late. The water went inside him and wouldn't let go. His arms and legs didn't want to move.

Bubbles came out of his mouth and he watched them float past his nose. The sun started going out.

~~~

Ray hit the bottom of the stairs in his stocking feet as Benny went under. The pirate hat popped to the surface like a bobber. The boys cheered and swam off with it and the sword. Ray lunged through the iron gate to the pool and dove in.

Benny wasn't breathing when Ray dragged him from the water. "God damn it, don't do this to me." He stretched his son out on the concrete and forced back the fear hammering through him. He wouldn't lose his son. Not like this. God damn it, not like this. He flashed on a scrawny boy standing over his best friend's body on the river bank. Some lady did CPR, but it was too late.

Ray tipped Benny's chin up, pinched his nose and blew two deep breaths into his mouth. No response. He laced his fingers, the palm of his left hand over the top of his right, and pumped Benny's chest with the heel of his hand, once, twice.

On the second compression, Benny coughed up water. Ray rolled him onto his side to keep him from choking.

"Is he gonna be okay?" One of the boys stood close enough that his orange swim trunks dripped pool water on Benny's head.

"Step back," Ray said. "Give him some air."

The boy did as told.

Benny struggled to sit up. Ray helped him, steadied his shoulders. "How you feelin', son?"

"My throat hurts."

"I bet it does."

The boy watching on said, "I thought all

pirates could swim." He looked to be about six years old, his narrow hips barely holding his swim trunks up. His lower lip trembled.

The adrenaline drained from Ray's muscles and he sat back on his heels. "Not this one." He'd been trying to teach Benny for two summers now, but coordination continued to be a problem. His son could do a lot of things, but learning not to breathe under water hadn't caught on yet.

The other boy, a head taller and wearing dark blue trunks, pushed forward and laid the pirate hat and sword next to Benny with great care. "Here's your stuff."

"Thank you," Benny mumbled.

"My little brother and me are sorry, mister. We was just playing a game."

Ray figured he should give the boys a lecture on pool safety, but he didn't have the strength or will. His son was alive. Nothing else mattered. "It's okay, boys," he said. "You two run along now."

He held his son in the shade of a patio umbrella, too weak to try standing. From where they sat, Ray saw the costume shop across the street, tucked between an auto parts outlet and a deli. A mannequin in the window wore the same hat that lay next to them at pool's edge. The memory of Virginia's voice washed over him.

Ray honey. You need to wake up now.

He fell asleep, the first good sleep he had in a long time, and Benny almost died because of it. His dead wife saved their son.

Grace appeared at his side, barefoot, hair disheveled, her warm brown skin gray with concern. "You boys alright?"

"Yeah," Benny answered.

"Ray?"

He guessed he was about as far from alright as a man could get. Grace must have seen it in his face. She reached out and smoothed his wet hair back from his forehead, like a mother would do a son. The gesture felt so good it almost brought tears to his eyes.

"Let's get you boys into some dry clothes."

~~~

Before leaving Santa Fe, they found a Laundromat to dry Ray and Benny's wet things. Grace had seen her share, traveling with Papa. At least this one was clean, and except for the pale, listless woman sitting in the far corner, her head drooped over a magazine, they had the place to themselves. Grace kept one eye on the door, on the chance they'd been followed, and the other on her traveling companions. Ray sat with his arm around Benny's shoulders, staring at the dryer as though mesmerized by their tumbling clothes. He looked like a man with only one screw left holding him together, his skin bleached whiter than natural.

"When we get back on the road," Grace said, "why don't you let me drive for a while? Benny can be my copilot while you stretch out in back and take a nap."

He didn't answer. Grace thought maybe he hadn't heard her over the noise of the dryer and the listless woman's washer thumping into its spin cycle. "Ray honey?"

He jerked and gave her a haunted look that put a fright in her. When he spoke, his low voice sounded course as sandpaper. "I'm not sleeping."

Grace knew better than to argue the point. His son nearly drowned. It would be a long time before he could forgive himself. She remembered the time a stranger came to her door, towing five-year-old Eddy junior by the arm and claiming he had to swerve into a trash can to avoid hitting the child. She'd been in the basement, pulling a load of sheets from the washer to hang on the line. The stranger shamed her for not keeping a closer eye on her children. The memory still sent shivers up her arms.

And with it, another memory shook loose. Her phone number came to her as clear as if somebody wrote it in flame-red lipstick on the dryer door. It brought her to her feet.

"I need to step out for a minute and find a pay phone," she said, pressing her purse to her bosom. "Can I get you boys anything?"

"A cup of coffee would be nice," Ray said. "Son, how 'bout you?"

"Beer, please."

Grace blinked.

"He means a root beer." The corner of Ray's mouth tipped in a half-hearted smile. "Guess he saw the burger place across the way."

That half-hearted smile eased some of Grace's concern about the man's mental state. "Coffee and beer it is," she said, and started for the door. "I won't be long."

13: The Second Rescue

The dryer buzzed and their clothes stopped moving. Benny popped up, "Got it," and yanked open the dryer door. Hot air whooshed across his head. He grabbed the clothes and pushed his face into them. They smelled like swimming pool water and reminded him that he almost died. Nobody said those words to him, but he knew. He felt bad that he made his daddy scared. It scared him too, at first, not being able to breathe. But then it got dark and quiet. Peaceful. Was that how it felt to Mama?

"Bring 'em over here, son."

His dad stood by a long, high table. Benny had never been in a place like this before, but he'd seen them in the movies. He thought it was cool that somebody put everything you needed to do the wash all in one big room, even a table to lay your clothes on to fold. The washers and dryers and soap machines reminded him of an arcade where you put quarters in slots, except he understood how things worked better here than in an arcade. It smelled like their laundry room at home – dirty socks and soap powder that made him sneeze.

The lady with the magazine put her clothes in a dryer and went outside to smoke a cigarette. Benny couldn't see her because she leaned against the other side of the wall, but her smoke puffed past the open door.

Grace should be back soon. He checked his scuba-diver watch, glad it still worked after going swimming, but he didn't remember what time Grace left. He worried about her, that she got across the street okay, that nobody bothered her. Watching the cigarette smoke made him feel funny inside, like it was trying to tell him something but he didn't know what. He pulled his black t-shirt from the clothes pile, laid it flat on the table and smoothed the wrinkles out of the Terminator's motorcycle. Daddy would have a big, black motorcycle some day. It was one of those things he knew without being able to explain it.

That made him think of Grace again. A

phone rang and he jumped.

"It's outside somewheres," his dad said as he folded his jeans.

The phone rang again and Benny got an awful feeling in his stomach. "Answer."

"Son, it ain't – " Daddy stopped and gave that frown he got when he all-of-a-sudden remembered something or couldn't figure something out. This time Benny thought it might be a little of both.

The phone rang again and Daddy hurried for the door.

~~~

Where's Grace?

"You stay put," Ray yelled over his shoulder.

The midday sun glared off the windshield of the Olds as he stepped outside. The woman having a smoke must have bused or walked to the Laundromat because the Olds sat alone in the parking lot. The pay phone, mounted to the far corner of the building, continued to ring. Ray got a sick feeling in his stomach when he realized how close the phone was and how long Grace had been gone. Smoker woman stood between him and it. She snubbed her cigarette on the concrete with the toe of her flip flop and reached for the receiver.

"No!"

The woman jerked back like he'd slapped her hand. "Well, excuse me," she said and pushed by him to go inside.

Ray's hand shook as he lifted the receiver to his ear. "Hello?"

"You the guy with my money?"

Ray couldn't have recognized the voice of the caller as belonging to the car-thieving weasel he decked back in Springer because he hadn't given the asshole an opportunity to speak, but he didn't doubt it for an instant. He swallowed hard, felt sweat pool in his armpits. "That depends."

"Don't get cute," the caller drawled. "There's a rest stop just off the Interstate, south of town. Be there with my money if you wanna see Granny again."

Ray stiffened. "She's not – "

The asshole hung up.

~~~

His dad hurried back inside, body all stiff, fists tight at his sides, and Benny knew something happened to Grace. The bad man happened to her. Benny knew the bad man would cause more trouble.

Daddy's color halo burned like fire. "That car-thieving weasel took Grace."

"We'll save her," Benny said.

"Damn straight we will. We're going to give the guy his money back and be done with this crap. Grab the clothes and let's get out of here."

Benny didn't argue. He had a plan.

~~~

Ray found the rest stop where the caller said it would be. The red Mustang Boss 302 with blacked-out hood, slatted rear window, and rear deck spoiler – a '69, if Ray knew his classic muscle cars – stood out like a lone neon sign, parked in front of the public restrooms. Ray didn't see anybody else around. No Grace. No asshole. Not even a fellow traveler stopped to take a leak.

"Where are they?" he wondered aloud.

Benny didn't answer. When Ray said they were going to give the money back, his son pulled inside himself. It made Ray uncomfortable, but he didn't have time to worry on it right now.

He parked several spaces away from the Mustang. "Stay put," he ordered, and got out.

As soon as he took a step away from the Olds, Grace stumbled around the corner of the building, shoved from behind by the scrawny man in the ugly black and white striped shirt. It appeared he had Grace's arms bound behind her back. Her purse hung from her neck and rested on her bosom. Her abductor shoved her ahead of him a few more steps, until they stood broadside of the Mustang, then jerked her to a halt.

If it hadn't been for Grace's messed up hair and tight expression, Ray would have found it amusing that she stood a couple inches taller than the guy and outweighed him by more than a few pounds. Though still several yards away, Ray could make out the guy's fat lower lip below the cigarette dangling from the corner of his mouth. His right eye looked swollen, too. Ray didn't recall hitting him there.

When he met Grace's gaze, her chin bumped up a notch as if to assure him she still had some fight left in her. Ray guessed she leaned against the man a little heavier than need be for support, making him work to keep her hostage.

"You okay?" Ray called.

"Save the chit chat," Mustang man shouted. "Give me the bag and I let your grandma here go."

Ray clenched his fists. "She's my friend, asshole. If you hurt her – "

"You'll what? Sic the dummy pirate on me?"

From the direction the man jerked his chin,

Ray knew without turning that Benny had gotten out and stood near the front of the Olds. In the steadiest voice he could muster, he called, "Stay back, son."

No response. Still, Ray didn't turn to see if Benny heard, much less obeyed. He kept his attention focused on Grace and the man blowing cigarette smoke over her shoulder. As the cloud wafted across her face, Grace's nose wrinkled and her brows drew even tighter. Her knees sagged, causing her abductor to stagger against the added weight. He must have poked her in the back, because she flinched and straightened. But Ray knew she hadn't straightened all the way because she and the man behind her were now the same height.

And she still had that severe look of disapproval on her face.

Easy, Ray silently warned. He didn't know what kind of weapon Mustang man had and he didn't want to find out the hard way. "How do we do this?" he shouted.

"Tell dummy boy to bring the bag over to me. Then I'll let your *friend* go."

Grace yanked against the man's hold. "That boy's smarter than *you'll* ever be," she snapped.

For a second, Ray thought she might pull

free, but the little weasel stuck to her like a leach. Ray decided to end this before somebody got hurt. "Bring me the bag," he called to Benny.

"No, Dad."

Ray saw Grace's face slacken, as though in shock. His stomach clenched and he turned to see Benny come around the car, pirate hat low on his forehead, plastic sword hanging from his waist, the Smith & Wesson raised in a two-handed hold.

"Ben. No." His voice sounded as if it came from miles away. He remembered taking the rounds out of his shirt pocket and stowing them in his suitcase at the motel in Santa Fe. Did Benny get into his suitcase while he slept and reload the gun? He had time to walk across the street, buy a pirate costume and go for a swim, so why not? Ray had no way of telling from where he stood if the gun was loaded. Did his son even know how to load a revolver?

A betting man would put money on the pirate.

"Son, give me the gun." Ray held out his hand, disconcerted to see it shaking. He took a cautious step toward the boy.

Benny advanced three more paces, then

adopted a spread-legged stance and aimed. The scene should have been comical – a pirate in a western-style showdown, like somebody spliced the wrong movies together – but Ray had never seen his son look more serious. And from the new angle, he could see the base of the cartridges in the gun's cylinder.

"Ben – "

"Let her go," the boy ordered, his voice stronger and deeper than Ray thought possible for an eleven-year-old.

"Tell the dummy to – "

"Stop calling him that!"

Ray watched in amazement as Grace elbowed Mustang man hard in the gut, then spun out and away from him. Without the use of her arms for balance, she tripped over her feet and landed on her side in the grass at the edge of the building.

Mustang man stood exposed, clutching his gut with one hand and holding what looked like a small pocket knife in the other.

"Dad, get Grace."

"Give me the gun first."

"Stop playin' games and give me my damn money!" Mustang man shouted. He and Ray both started toward Benny at the same time.

"Get down!"

It was the boy's best Schwarzenegger impression yet – *get dowwwn* – and Ray froze. The movie scene flashed into his head, the Terminator hip-shooting the pistol-grip shotgun. Helpless, he realized Benny was going to shoot an instant before the revolver bucked.

The concussion hammered Ray's eardrums. He made a lunge for the gun but it bucked again and a sharp burn across his right shoulder drove him back against the open door of the Olds. The door gave. With nothing to grab onto, Ray couldn't stop his backward slide down the side of the car. He landed on his ass, jarring his tailbone hard enough to slam his teeth together. Benny fired the remaining four rounds.

It took a couple seconds for Mustang man, tucked into a low squat, arms folded over his head, to realize the shooting had stopped. He looked at Benny, seemed satisfied the gun was empty, then straightened and patted his chest, as though surprised to find himself in one piece. The knife lay at his feet, but the cigarette still dangled from his mouth as if glued there.

Benny had missed the man with every shot. Ray counted five holes in the rear quarter-panel of the Mustang. Not bad shooting, five out of six. It dawned on him that the boy never intended to shoot the "bad man," just blow up his car, like he saw it done in the movies.

But this wasn't the movies.

~~~

Benny stared in disbelief, the gun heavy at his side. *Why didn't the car blow up? In the movies the car always blows up!* He must have done it wrong. But now he didn't have anymore bullets and he couldn't try again. He didn't know what to do.

Stupid boy!

~~~

Ray noticed the puddle forming behind the Mustang's rear tire. Benny had punctured the gas tank. Mustang man saw the holes in the quarter-panel and shouted something at Benny, but Ray couldn't make it out over the concussive ringing in his ears. Not that it mattered. As the owner of a classic muscle car, it pained Ray to see the cherry 'Stang shot up that way.

Mustang man yanked the cigarette from his mouth – so it wasn't glued in after all – and tossed it behind him as he advanced. It was a good toss. The cigarette covered the distance between him and the car and landed in the pool of gas.

Ray muttered "oh crap," and waited for the explosion.

14: The Missing Bullet

The cigarette fizzled out.

Ray used the door handle to pull himself to his feet. His right shoulder smarted, but his ass hurt worse, like he'd been mule kicked. He shouldn't have been surprised the cigarette didn't send the Mustang up in flames. That only happened in the movies, too. Gritting his teeth, he made an effort to stand straight. *Time to get the hell outta Dodge.*

Grace did a crazy run-walk towards the Olds, her hands still tied behind her, her purse bouncing in rhythm with her bosom. Ray did a hobbling run-walk of his own, each step a knife of pain radiating from his tailbone. Benny didn't resist when Ray took the gun from him, shoved him around to the passenger side of the car and into the back. Grace piled in after, landing sideways on the front seat. Ray dropped the gun on the floor at her feet, slammed the door shut and turned. Mustang man stood an arm's length away.

Ray swung.

His fist found its target. He felt the cartilage in Mustang man's nose crunch. The man staggered back, blood oozing from both nostrils, his eyes wide, as though shocked he'd been hit again. The guy was dumber than he looked, Ray concluded, then winced as the weasel caught the curb with his heel and sat down hard on the concrete sidewalk. *Man, I know how* that *feels*.

No time to share bruised tailbone stories. Ray hobble-ran around the back of the Olds to the driver's side and grabbed the gym bag from behind the seat.

"Dad!"

He ignored his son's protest and gave the bag a left-handed, sideways toss over the hood of the car. To his astonishment, it landed neatly in Mustang man's lap.

Ray shouted, "Take your money and leave us the hell alone!"

Without waiting for a response, he got behind the wheel of the Olds and endured another sharp stab to his sit-bone that went clear to his teeth. His right hand throbbed as he reached for the keys dangling in the ignition. The engine gunned to life.

Grace lay half on her side in the seat next to him. Her hair looked like a flock of birds had nested in it and a huge grass stain ran the length of one purple sleeve.

Relief and something close to love flooded through Ray. "Are you alright?"

She squirmed herself up straighter in the seat and pulled free of her binding – what looked like the leather strap from a camera case. "I'm fine," she replied, "but you're bleeding."

He followed her gaze to the growing stain on the ragged shoulder of his t-shirt, felt an uncomfortable tug in his stomach. The sight of his own blood did that to him. He looked away. He had an idea what happened but didn't have the time or inclination to dwell on it right now. The sorry weasel with the bloody nose and shot-up Boss 302 wasn't much of a threat at this point, but Ray couldn't be sure all the shooting hadn't attracted attention from the Interstate. He didn't plan to stick around for the police to show up.

"I'll worry about it later," he said, and threw the Olds into reverse.

~~~

Grace took her purse from around her neck and gave the road atlas a quick study. "We should get off the Interstate. Take Highway 14 to Cerrillos."

He did as she said without question. Once he had them headed south, Ray commented, "You seem to know a lot about evading the law."

"Never the law. No, sir. We were careful to stay on the right side of that. But Papa could spot a crooked move at the card table nine ways to Sunday – base deals, hangers, false shuffling. He wouldn't let on he knew 'bout it, just proceeded to beat the cheat at his own game. It didn't set well with some." She carried the scar of one such encounter, the only time she ever saw her papa pull his derringer on a man.

"I bet you have a lot of interesting stories to tell."

"That I do." And she prayed every day to hang onto them until she breathed her last. She gave a short laugh. "Now I can add being kidnapped to the lot."

Ray didn't appear to find it as amusing. "Damn it, Grace. I'm sorry as hell we got you mixed up in this. If that weasel hurt you – "

159

"Hush that talk. I'm just glad you boys showed up when you did, else I might've had to black his other eye."

Ray cocked a brow at her. "You did that?"

"His face got in the way of my elbow whilst tying me up. Only reason he got me in his car is 'cause the coward caught me from behind." Put his greasy hand over her mouth and breathed sour cigarettes in her face when he told her to shut up and not make it worse for herself. All the while poking at her with his pathetic pocketknife. She dug through her purse for a packet of tissues. "His name's Johnny. Least that's what he told me. The money is a gambling debt."

"Did he tell you why he left it in a garbage can?"

"Didn't get a chance to ask." She didn't need to. A man desperate enough to resort to kidnapping had to be in debt to a dangerous sort. "He got what he was after, that's all that matters." And why she played along with the abduction. She could have broke free any number of times once she got her wits about her. But she wanted this business over. Now that the money was back with its rightful owner, they could get on to Las Vegas.

She found the tissues, took the entire

contents from the wrapper, pulled Ray's t-shirt collar aside and pressed the makeshift dressing to his wound, causing him to draw in a sharp breath.

"Stings a mite," he said.

"I s'pect it does." Most of the bleeding had stopped, but if the injury was from what she thought, they would need to guard against infection. "Do you have a first aid kit?"

"There's one in the trunk."

"Best find a place to park so's we can get this taken care of proper."

Some of the color drained from Ray's face. "Did I catch the missing bullet?"

"Looks that way."

~~~

Ray guessed as much, but Grace's confirmation meant he could no longer ignore the fact that his son shot him. A couple inches to the left and it might have been fatal. He glanced in the rearview mirror and saw the crocodile tears rolling down Benny's stricken face. "I'm okay, son. It was an accident. The bullet musta ricocheted off something." He looked over at Grace for help. "It's not as bad as it looks, right?"

"Just a scratch," she replied, her tone almost cheery.

Somehow her response did nothing to settle his queasy stomach.

~~~

Benny knew what his dad planned to do when he stopped the car on the side of the road, told them "this won't take long," and got out. Grace must have known too because she just nodded and watched him walk away.

"Lord Jesus, look after that man," she said in a quiet voice.

Amen, Benny thought. He remembered the time when Daddy tried to put Christmas lights on the outside of the house and fell backwards off the ladder. He landed on his butt and walked funny for a while. That's how he walked now. Benny didn't understand how getting shot in the shoulder could make your butt hurt, but he decided not to ask Daddy or Grace to explain. He didn't want to talk about what happened at the rest stop, in case somebody asked him a question he didn't want to answer.

He never wanted to see the gun again. It hurt his ears and tried to jump out of his hands when he pulled the trigger. The hot smell burned his nose. Shooting wasn't anything like he saw in the movies.

Lots of things happened different than in the

movies. It confused him. But even if the shiny red car didn't blow up, it didn't have any gas left in it, so the bad man couldn't follow them now. The money –

"Sugar?"

He blinked and saw Grace looking at him. She handed him the car keys. "I'm going to check on your daddy. Would you please get the first aid kit from the trunk?"

"'kay."

~~~

Grace groaned at the stiffness in her joints as she climbed out of the car. She hit the ground hard back at the rest stop, tripping over her fool feet that way. Lucky I didn't break anything, she thought, remembering Mr. Stuart's wife, Dot, and her broke toe from gardening. Escaping a kidnapper certainly made a more interesting story. Her blouse was ruined. First her church hat, and now her beautiful open-neck poplin with pearlized buttons. If she weren't careful, she'd need to buy a new wardrobe before long.

She found Ray on his hands and knees in the shade of a pinyon tree a few yards from the car. The gun rested in a hole he had carved in the dirt. He clutched the stub of a stick in one fisted hand. He didn't move at her approach, his back stiff as a pine board.

Grace gave a soft grunt and one ankle popped as she squatted next to him. Getting back up could present a problem. "You don't have to do this," she said, putting a hand on Ray's shoulder. "The child won't touch that gun again after what's happened."

"It's best this way," he said, his voice tight as his posture.

Grace remembered the regret she felt over selling her papa's derringer, like selling a piece of his life. "Has it been in your family long?"

"Naw." He shook his head, then winced.

"What's troubling you, Ray?"

"I can't get up."

"Your back go out on you?"

"My ass."

Grace yanked her hand away. "Pardon me?"

"I fell on it when I got shot. Hurts like a sombitch." His shoulders shook and she realized he was laughing in spite of the pain it caused. He lifted the stub of stick. "And I broke my damn shovel."

Grace snorted. "I'll find you a new one."

~~~

Back at the Olds, Ray worked his t-shirt off, pulling the bottom up and sliding his left arm out first. Grace soaked a gauze pad from a bottle of water and washed the torn skin at his collarbone. Just a scratch, like she said. But it stung like hell.

"'kay, Dad?"

His son looked on the verge of tears again. "Fine as frog's hair," Ray said and Benny smiled.

Ray did his best to keep from flinching as Grace applied a fresh gauze pad smeared with antibiotic cream. Benny handed him a clean white t-shirt and he pulled it on, mindful of his right shoulder. He wadded the gauze used to wash his wound inside his bloody shirt. "Son, get me that plastic bag we been using for garbage?"

"Yeah."

While Benny went for the bag on the back floor of the Olds, Ray turned to Grace. Keeping his voice low, he said, "If it's alright with you, I think we'll stay off the Interstate awhile longer."

"You expecting more trouble?"

"Can't say for sure." He glanced at Benny's waggling backside. "But something ain't right."

Grace snapped the first aid kit shut. "I'll get the atlas."

~~~

Highway 14, The Turquoise Trail, more or

less paralleled Interstate 25, beginning just south of Santa Fe and ending at Interstate 40, east of Albuquerque. They made it as far as the Cerrillos turnoff, when Ray announced, "I gotta stop and walk around some."

Weathered-board and adobe buildings lined dirt streets; a hitching rail out front of Mary's Bar; and across the way, the bell tower and dome of a Catholic church poked through the trees. Grace felt like she'd been transported onto an Old West movie set.

"There," Benny said, pointing to the Casa Grande Trading Post. Rusted mining equipment and bins of rocks crowded for space outside a long, low building with windows full of old bottles and glass powerline insulators.

"Looks good to me," Ray said. "Grace?"

"I could use me a stretch."

More bins of rocks and minerals filled the interior, squeezed between shelves of polished gem stones and cases of turquoise and jewelry, labeled boxes of antique barbed wire and railroad spikes, antlers, Civil War era bullets, pueblo pottery. Dust hovered in the afternoon sun filtering through green, blue and brown glass displayed in the windows.

Grace bought a smooth hematite stone the size of a quarter. Benny bought a bag of feed for the Petting Zoo in back. As he snapped pictures of llamas, goats and rabbits, Grace sidled up close to Ray and asked, "Does he have any film in that thing?"

"Naw. They don't make that kind anymore."

She went back inside and bought the boy a disposable 35mm camera.

"Thank you, honey," he said, and snapped her picture.

Grace raised a hand to the scarf she'd tied around her hair. The smell of cigarettes and Johnny's cheap cologne clung to her skin and clothes. "I need to find someplace to wash up and change," she declared.

"And I could eat the south end of a north bound cow," Ray stated.

Benny patted his stomach. "Me too."

The owner of the Trading Post recommended a place in Madrid – he pronounced it MAD-rid – just south of Cerrillos. Three miles later, they entered an artsy gallery community and located the cafe.

Grace said, "You boys order me something good. I'll be a few minutes," and headed for the women's bathroom, lugging her suitcase with her.

When she came out fifteen minutes later wearing an airy teal blouse and denim capris, her hair smoothed into a high bun and wrapped in a bright batik scarf, Benny said, "Nice," and grinned.

Grace gave a silent prayer of thanks for the pork enchiladas, rhubarb pie, mint tea and endless coffee, served outside on a patio shaded by a broad cottonwood tree. A warm afternoon breeze soughed through the leaves and brushed her face. The smell of mint when she raised her glass to her mouth soothed her nerves. She watched the methodic way Benny ate one thing at a time and wiped his mouth with his napkin often. Ray's subtle shift in his seat every few minutes. The feeling that divine hands had guided her here, to Madrid, New Mexico, and the best rhubarb pie she'd had since Jolie Johnston passed away – God rest her soul – hummed through her strong.

Benny looked up from his pie and Grace caught the word content. She acknowledged his message with a smile and he returned to his pie. Grace reached for her tea, had the glass almost to her lips, when another thought pinged in her head. Her hand stilled.

I never called my husband.

15: Preacher Man

Dear Lord, give me strength to be honest and forthright with my man, Grace prayed as she lifted the pay phone's receiver and began pushing buttons. *Please let this be the right number.*

"Grace? Honey, is that you?"

Relief whooshed through her, followed close by guilt at the worry she heard in her husband's voice. "Yes, dear, it's me."

"Praise Jesus, where are you?" Then, "You've been gone since Sunday."

"What's today?" she asked, before thinking how it might sound.

"Tuesday." Ed's voice went flat and careful. "Grace, what's going on?"

Tuesday?

"Grace!"

"I'm here," she said in a rush. "I be fine."

"Why'd you call sister instead of me? She said – "

"I couldn't remember our phone number," Grace cut in, her tone impatient.

The line went quiet for a few seconds. "Do you know where you are?"

"Madrid, New Mexico," she said, then answered before he asked, "I'm on my way to Las Vegas."

She heard an abrupt grunt and exhale, as though he dropped onto one of their kitchen chairs hard enough to knock the wind out of himself. "Is this about the Stardust casino?"

"You found the newspaper article."

"I did."

"Remember the story I told you about Papa and me?"

"Of course I do."

"I don't." She shook her head, rubbed at the sharp twinge in her temple. "I mean...I didn't. Until I read the headline. Eddy, I have to see the Stardust 'fore I forget again...'fore it's gone."

"You could have talked to me about it instead of running off."

And he would have talked her out of going, most likely. But that didn't matter now. "I wasn't thinking straight."

"Did you have one of your attacks?"

Doctor Medford and his panic attacks. She didn't much care for the idea of being a panicky old woman, but how else could she explain her erratic behavior?

Her husband didn't wait for an answer. "Do you know anything about Leeta's car?"

"I borrowed it and it broke down on the Interstate. I tried to tell her, but she wouldn't hold that tongue of hers long enough to get a word in edgewise."

"They found it west of Conroy. How'd you get to New Mexico? How're you getting to Vegas?"

"These nice folks stopped to help and offered to give me a ride."

"Nice folks? Gracie...?"

"Oh, Eddy, you'd understand if you met them. Ray's a widower, wife died sudden in her sleep, left a boy with Down syndrome missin' his mama something awful. You know how the Lord works in mysterious ways, honey. It's like God put me in their path so's I can help them through their grief." It was the best she could do over the phone.

She heard him draw in a long breath, giving himself time to think before speaking, a habit she knew well. A habit she respected in her man. "'God works for the good of those who love Him,'" he said, pulling a passage from the bible. Another brief pause. "I trust your judgment, honey. Do you know how you're getting home?"

"I'll buy me a bus ticket and call you when I know my schedule. I love you, Eddy. I have to go now."

"I love you too, Gracie. I pray the Lord's hand guides you back home safe."

She hung up and turned from the pay phone to find Benny standing beside her. He put his arms around her middle in a hug. Grace rested her cheek on his head and breathed in the smell of perspiration and chlorine. Was it just this morning the child nearly drowned? Events jumbled in her mind.

Tuesday?

Benny squeezed her hard and said, "Don't worry," his words muffled in her bosom. He tipped his head back to look up at her, his almond-shaped eyes earnest. "We'll take care of you."

He spoke slow, enunciating as well as his physical limitations allowed. Grace understood. The compassion in his expression, his conviction. Her unease subsided. "I know you will, sugar. Thank you."

The boy grinned, a blush coloring his cheeks. Grace planted a kiss on his forehead. "Let's get your daddy. We got miles to cover."

~~~

The Turquoise Trail turned out to be some pretty country, hillier, the Sandia Mountains in the distance – according to Grace's study of the road atlas. But Ray was happy to be back on I-40, headed west. He drove into the mid-afternoon sun, window rolled down, elbow resting on the sill, the ache in his tailbone bearable for the time being.

Grace stowed the atlas and gazed out the passenger window, drawn into her thoughts. She didn't say anything about the call she made in Madrid, but he could see it weighed on her. He didn't ask; it wasn't his business. Benny sat in the middle of the rear seat, smoking a crayon cigarette, pirate hat tipped back, his Terminator sunglasses sliding down his nose. Ray wondered how this trip would have played out if not for the kid's love of movies. Probably boring as all get-out. Hell, they might never have left Beavercreek without Thelma and Louise's help. And he sure wouldn't have got shot. He smiled to himself and added a couple more notches to their speed.

A few minutes later he heard a metallic rattle from under the hood of the Olds. He glanced at the dash gauges and saw the oil pressure dropping fast.

"Crap."

"What is it?" Grace asked.

"We're losing oil." The rattle became a hammering knock and Ray signaled to pull over. As he reached for the ignition key, the engine gave a bone-jarring *Bang!* and died.

Benny thrust his head between the seats. "What happened?"

"We're overheated?" Grace offered.

Ray wished it could be that simple. "I'll take a look," he said. "You two wait here."

He checked for traffic and got out. Once he lifted the hood, it didn't take long to find the fist-size hole in the engine block. A blown rod. Oil covered the stock gold engine and pooled on the road. Defeat tightened Ray's chest. His mint condition Burgundy Mist '69 Olds 442 was dead.

Damn it, God, what more do you want from me?

The anger he held in check since his wife's death heaved through him. He wanted to lash out, vent on God, vent on himself. He fisted his bruised right hand and pain shot up his forearm, compliments of Johnny's bony face.

Impotence blurred his vision and he took a clumsy swing at the underside of the hood with his left.

A horn blared. Ray saw a pickup swerve into the center lane as it blasted by the Olds. The driver flipped him the bird. Ray flipped a left-handed finger back. He seemed to be ambidextrous at that skill, at least. He heard the driver's side door of the Olds shut and realized Benny had tried to get out. No doubt to see if his dad was okay.

Don't lose it now, Ray told himself.

He took a deep breath, rolled his head to loosen the tightness in his neck, then walked away from the open hood. Climbing behind the steering wheel, he said, "Looks like we're gonna have to hitch a ride into Albuquerque."

Benny plopped back in his seat. "Oh, man."

"Can it be repaired?" Grace asked.

"With a lot of time and money. Both of which we don't have."

"I'm sorry, Ray. I know how much this car means to you."

"Yeah, well," he said, unable look her in the eye, "it's just a car. Let's get our bags out of the trunk and our thumbs in the air."

~~~

Benny didn't have room in his suitcase for

his cowboy hat, so he got his dad to wear it. His sword wouldn't fit in the suitcase either, and he sure didn't want to leave it behind for somebody to steal, so he hooked the plastic sheath to his belt. Dad started to say something, then shook his head and pulled their suitcases out of the trunk. Benny reached for a sleeping bag.

"We're not going to need those," Dad said.

"For the Grand Canyon," Benny explained and reached for the second bag. He knew his dad didn't think they'd get to the Grand Canyon now that the car was broken, so it was up to him to be the strong one and do the straight thinking.

Dad sighed and took the sleeping bags from him. Benny reached for the tent.

"No, son, we're not packin' that thing around."

Benny frowned. "Yeah, we need – "

"I'll carry it," Grace said, taking it from him.

"Aw, hell, why don't we take the fishing gear too," Dad snapped.

"Don't use that tone with me," Grace snapped back. "If the boy feels we need these things, then we're taking them."

Dad stared hard at her but she put her straw hat on and ignored him. Benny tried not to smile.

"Guess I'm out-numbered," Dad grumbled.

"Guess so," Grace answered. She hung her purse on her shoulder, straightened her hat and grabbed her suitcase in one hand and the tent in the other.

Dad got ready to close the trunk. "Anything else before I lock up?"

Benny shook his head. They had everything they needed to finish their trip.

~~~

A feeling of déjà vu washed over Grace as she stood on the shoulder of I-40, a dead car behind her, the afternoon sun baking the tops of her feet through her thin canvas shoes, the gritty air heavy with the smell of exhaust and hot tires. She may as well be back in Arkansas instead of the middle of New Mexico. Except this time she wasn't in a panic and the car on the side of the Interstate wasn't stolen.

A stout breeze caught the long, narrow tent bag, swung it around and nearly twisted it out of her grip. She had no idea why she offered to carry the silly thing, other than to avoid more tension in an already tense situation. Her purse strap dug into her shoulder. She squished her hat down tight to keep it from blowing off in the wind kicked up by passing traffic. Ray stood beside her, a suitcase in one hand, a sleeping bag in the other. The cowboy hat fit him better than it did his son, the brim shading his eyes and giving him a bit of a Clint Eastwood squint. Benny stood next to him with his own suitcase and the other sleeping bag, his three-pointed hat sitting at a jaunty angle – a hitchhiking pirate in cargo shorts and a Terminator t-shirt.

Grace couldn't help it. She took in the picture they made, the three of them together, and laughed.

Benny and Ray looked at her like she'd lost her mind.

"Ain't we a sight," she said.

Benny grinned.

A slow smile drew one side of Ray's mouth up. "Yeah, I suppose we are."

"Think we'll have to stand out here long?"

"Not long." He looked over her shoulder as he spoke.

Grace turned to see an orange tractor trailer rig slowing, its right signal flashing.

~~~

Ray held Benny back as the truck geared down and came to a stop on the shoulder. A massive woman in tennis shoes, tight jeans and a traffic-stopping yellow tank top slid out of the passenger side, her short, blonde ponytail whipping to keep up with her.

"Hey, folks," she hollered over the truck engine's idle. "Car trouble?"

"Yes, ma'am," Ray called, moving closer. Benny and Grace followed. "Mind giving us a lift to Albuquerque?" Ponytail had arms the size of hams. Not fat – what Virginia would have generously called big-boned. Ray figured the woman could give a lift to damn near anything she'd a mind to.

"Be our pleasure. Hop in."

Benny brushed by Ray to go first. He scrambled into the cab with ham woman's help. Then she tossed his suitcase and sleeping bag up to him. "Just put your things on the bed there!" she hollered.

Grace climbed in next, also with a boost from those huge arms. Ray attempted to climb in unassisted, but a sharp stab of pain in his tailbone caught him halfway up. The pause must have been long enough for ham woman to decide he needed help too, and the next thing he knew, he found himself launched into the truck. Benny had already stretched out in the sleeper with his arms folded behind his head and his pirate hat tipped over his eyes. Ray sat next to Grace on the edge of the mattress.

The driver, a wiry-looking fellow in a blue t-shirt and Mariner's ball cap, twisted in his seat and extended his hand. "Name's Sam. This here's my wife, Pammy."

Ray bit the inside of his cheek and tried hard not to think about Sammy and his hammy wife Pammy as he shook the man's hand. "I'm Ray, the pirate's my son Benny, and our friend Grace."

"You folks been on the road long?" Sam asked.

"Ohio!" Benny shouted over Ray's shoulder.

"That's a few miles. Let's see if we can add a few more." Sam turned his attention to getting them back on the Interstate.

As the truck's engine accelerated and decelerated, the transmission sliding through its gears, Ray watched the Olds recede in the side mirror and felt another piece of himself die.

~~~

"Grace," Pammy said and turned to look at her. "That name's familiar. Have we met before?"

Grace knew her memory wasn't what it used to be, but she thought she'd remember this woman if their paths had crossed. "I'm sorry, but I don't believe so."

"I could swear..." Pammy frowned. "Have you been on TV lately?"

"No." Though for some reason the woman's question made her think of Ed. *What did he do?*

"Well," Pammy faced forward, "it'll come to me by and by."

Grace didn't think she wanted the woman to remember. She glanced at Ray and saw the pain in his face. "Is it your tailbone?" she asked, her voice low.

He shook his head. Grace followed his gaze to the passenger side mirror in time to see the burgundy speck of his car disappear behind a slight rise. "Oh." She patted his hand where it gripped the edge of the bed between them.

"I've got it!" the huge woman whooped.

Grace jumped, her hand flying to her bosom.

Pammy turned with triumph in her eyes. "You're that missing preacher's wife!"

Grace stared at her, too stunned to respond.

"Missing?" Ray asked. From her peripheral vision, Grace saw him watching her.

"Your face has been all over the news," Pammy informed them. "Mrs. Grace Brown, missing since Sunday afternoon, feared disoriented and lost."

"I'm not lost," Grace said.

Pammy hooted. "Maybe you should tell your husband that."

"Goddammit, Grace. You're a runaway?"

Her back stiffened and she looked sharp at Ray. "I'm no such thing! And stop using the Lord's name in vain."

"Then why doesn't your husband know where you are?" he asked.

It took her a second to stop opening and closing her mouth to answer. "I called him," she said, glancing away.

"When?"

"In Madrid."

"*Madrid?* Why'd you wait so long?"

She told him about not remembering her number and then remembering it wrong. "And then Johnny grabbed me before I could try again in Santa Fe."

"Aw hell." Ray lowered his voice. "I'm sorry, Grace."

The truth shall set you free. The bible passage taunted her. She could argue that Shakespeare's poor Emilia died for speaking the truth in *Othello*. But she weren't Emilia and it was time to clear her conscience. "There's more."

Ray stared at her, waiting.

"That wasn't my car you found me with."

Air whooshed from him as if she'd gut-punched him. *That's the second time today I've knocked the wind out of a man*. "You're a car thief?" Ray's voice got high and broke on "thief."

Grace tried desperately not to giggle.

"It isn't funny!" He ripped the cowboy hat from his head and threw it into the back of the sleeper.

Benny sat up behind them, his pirate hat pushed high, his smile wide. "Yeah, Dad, it is."

Grace could see Ray struggle. He wanted to nurse his anger, but the longer he chewed on it, the more the muscles in his face twitched.

"Whose car did you steal?"

"My sister-in-law's."

His burst of laughter exploded through the truck cab. He collapsed back against his son as though the emotional release sucked all the strength from his bones.

Sam bellowed, "Hot dog, Pammy, we're harboring us an outlaw!"

16: Hang On

Sam and Pammy dropped them off at a truck stop on the outskirts of Albuquerque. While Grace paid for two rooms at the motel next door, Ray called AAA to pick up the Olds and have it taken to a mechanic who specialized in classic American-made cars. When Ray announced he was headed to the shop – easy walking distance from the motel, as luck would have it – to discuss the repairs, Benny and Grace trooped over with him.

The estimate for a new engine block was staggering.

"Of course I'm going to have to order it," said the mechanic, a thick-waisted, fortyish man in blue coveralls and grease. "That'll take some time."

"How much time?"

"Three or four weeks probably."

Grace sighed, a painful sound, and went outside.

"We don't have three or four weeks," Ray said, keeping an eye on his friend through the shop's glass door. The stiff way Grace stood made her look fragile, like a gust of wind would shatter her. The full impact of her desperation to reach the Stardust in time hadn't hit him until this afternoon. She stole her sister-in-law's car to get there, for God's sake. Ray hadn't felt this protective of a woman since Gin. And he was letting her down. Never mind he only just met her Sunday afternoon. She had become more to him and his son in those two and a half days than he ever expected possible. She rode the same damn emotional rollercoaster he and Benny were on, headed for something just out of reach.

He didn't know how he was going to pay for the work on the Olds. He had a little money in –

"Dad?"

"Not now, son." Ray cleared his throat and met the mechanic's steady gaze. "Listen, we need to be in Nevada the day after tomorrow and I'm...well..."

Benny reached around him and laid a

bundle of twenties on the counter. Ray went speechless while his brain attempted to explain the money's presence. Of course it was Johnny's, but how did it get here? "What's in the bag?" he wondered aloud.

"Books."

Ray frowned. "Books?"

Benny gave an impatient huff. "In the motel room. Phone book. Bible."

"Aw, crap."

His son drew another bundle of twenties from a side pocket of his cargo shorts and laid it beside the first, lining them up on the counter so they formed a perfect rectangle. Ray's gaze jerked from the money to the mechanic – who continued to stare at the perfect rectangle of money – and wondered what might be going through the man's mind. Guilt, warranted or not, had Ray searching for an explanation that wouldn't make them out to be crooks or idiots. Both of which, if he thought on it too long, fit the bill.

The mechanic finally pried his eyes from the money and looked up. "I might have a solution to your problem, providing those greenbacks are real."

"Oh they're real," Ray muttered. "But we – "
Can't spend them, he intended to say, but his

son and the mechanic had already turned away and headed into the back of the shop, the money no longer on the counter.

~~~

Disappointment drained Grace. She wanted to cry but couldn't muster the strength. *I been actin' like a fool on a fool's journey*. The late afternoon heat pushed down on her shoulders and anchored her feet as though the souls of her shoes had melted to the sidewalk. The smell of dirty oil baking on concrete permeated from the shop's open rollup door a few feet away. Half a dozen cars waiting their turn for repair lined the chain-link fence surrounding the area. One looked like Ed's cream-yellow Lincoln, except somebody had painted flames up the side. Grace regretted not having the energy to be amused by the idea of her Eddy behind the wheel of something like that.

What am I going to do?

She had misplaced some of her money. There should have been more in her wallet when she pulled it out to help pay for a room at the truck stop motel. Replaying every step between Little Rock and hitching a ride with the trucker couple, Grace drew a blank.

Did I leave the waitress in Springer a whopper of a tip? Could two bills have stuck together when I paid for Benny's camera? Maybe I dropped some when I dug for change to call home.

The only thing she knew for certain was she couldn't afford to go forward and she couldn't afford to go back. She knew what her papa would have done, but that was too many years ago.

Lord Jesus, forgive me. Show me the way.

"How would you feel about riding in a sidecar?"

Grace jumped, the hairs on the back of her neck prickling. She looked up at the silly grin on Ray's face. "What on earth you talking about?"

Her snappish tone only made him grin wider. "Come with me and I'll show you."

She followed Ray into the mechanic's shop, around a sporty-looking blue car on a lift, past a rack of tools and fan belts and other parts foreign to Grace. The temperature cooled the deeper they went into the concrete space. There, tucked out of the way in a back corner, sat a gleaming black motorcycle with a sidecar.

"It's a Pearl Black Harley Davidson Softtail," Ray informed her. The reverence in his voice made him sound like a kid who just opened what he wanted most for Christmas.

"The Black Pearl," Benny said, squirming in

place like he had ants in his pants.

"What's gotten into you two?" Grace looked from father to son and back to father. "Whose motorcycle is this?"

"Mine," Ray said.

"I don't understand. Where'd you get the mon..." Her voice trailed off as realization settled in. "You didn't. Lord have mercy, tell me you didn't."

"I didn't," Ray assured her.

"I did," Benny said.

"I need to sit."

~~~

Ray knew he had no right to spend Johnny's money. The disbelief on Grace's face confirmed it. She leaned her rump against the Harley's saddle and looked at him like he'd lost his mind, like she'd never seen him before. Hell, he didn't recognize himself anymore either. Maybe he *had* lost his mind.

Blame it on the motorcycle. Not just any motorcycle – a Harley Davidson. When the mechanic – Andy was his name – uncovered the bike, Ray reeled against a flood of memories, the plans he and Gin made, the years spent talking about cross country travel once he retired. They could have taken the Olds, but he insisted a Harley was the only way to go, and he convinced Gin of it. At least she sounded willing enough, providing they didn't tent. He would never know for sure. Harleys were expensive. Time ran out.

Andy took the bike in trade for a 1968 Gran Torino GT, he told Ray. Now he needed to sell it to cover business expenses.

"You buy the bike," Andy said, "and I'll throw in the labor on your Olds for free."

Ray felt his resistance crumble. The mechanic's offer trumped any concerns over whose money he was spending. Destiny. That's what it felt like. Fate. No stopping the rollercoaster now.

Sit down, shut up and hang on.

He looked at Grace and said, "Trust me."

~~~

Grace did trust him. She had put her trust in him the moment they met. The haunted hope in his blue eyes as he waited for her approval decided it for her now. Whatever demons drove him, she had become a part of it, this journey that none of them seemed to have any control over. And God help her, she wanted to get to the Stardust before it ceased to exist.

The Lord will provide.

She straightened and said, "We're going to need riding gear."

~~~

Benny got the rest of the money from his suitcase to give to his dad to pay for their new motorcycle clothes. He was glad Dad didn't get mad when he found out the truth.

Dad let him "get outfitted" first. It took a long time to find leather pants big enough to go around his root beer belly but not too long so they had to be rolled up. Leather didn't roll up very good. He didn't have Mama to hem them for him, like she always did with his school pants. They finally found a pair that fit, though, and finding a jacket that fit was easy. Benny liked the way it smelled and made him feel tough. The big black boots were heavy. He practiced stomping around the store and decided they fit good too.

When Dad came out of the dressing room a little while later, wearing a black leather jacket and pants and boots, Benny sucked in a breath and whispered, "The Terminator."

Dad put on a pair of dark sunglasses. "Come with me if you want to live."

Just like in the movie. Excitement shivered through Benny.

Grace came out of the other dressing room, wearing her own black leather jacket, pants and boots. "I feel like a stuffed olive."

Dad snickered. Benny giggled, went to Grace and put his arm around her. "Looking good," he said. He meant it too. She looked tough, like she could stop bullets.

"Thank you, sugar." She gave him a squeeze. "Let's go pick out helmets 'fore anybody else sees me."

~~~

"You ever rode a bike with a sidecar?" Andy asked when they went back to pick up the Harley.

"Nope." Ray figured to steer instead of lean into turns. How hard could it be?

"Let's wheel it out back so you can practice," Andy offered.

A narrow blacktopped strip behind the building, an alleyway of sorts, ran the length of the block – buildings on the left, a chain-link fence and tall shrubs on the right. Ray swung his leg over the saddle, the motion causing his bruised tailbone to twinge a reminder, and started the engine. A thrill shot through him as the bike growled to life, the ache in his tailbone forgotten.

"Man, that sounds good," he shouted above the beefy rumble.

Andy grinned. "Who's your ballast?"

"My ballast?"

Grace stepped forward. "I think he means me."

"Climb on in," Andy said. "Be sure to fasten your seatbelt." He turned to Benny. "Go ahead and get on behind your dad. Might as well feel how the bike's gonna handle fully loaded."

Benny couldn't lift his leg high enough to clear the seat. Ray got off and helped him, then endured another sharp stab from his tailbone climbing back on.

"Take it slow at first," Andy warned. "She's gonna yaw."

Ray eased out on the clutch and the bike headed for the fence.

"Watch out!" Grace shouted.

Ray hit the brakes and the bike slued toward the building. Sweat popped out on his arms as he brought the Harley to a shaky stop.

"Thing to remember," Andy hollered, sprinting to catch up, "most of your weight's in the bike and driver, so the sidecar acts as a drag."

Now he tells me.

The band of Benny's arms around his waist made it hard to breathe. "Loosen up, son."

"'kay."

Ray took a breath and tried again. Prepared for the drag this time, he managed to keep the bike pointed straight. The front end began shimmying and he stopped again.

"That normal?" he asked when Andy caught up to them.

Andy nodded. "It'll smooth out once you pick up a little speed. Go ahead and take 'er around the side streets here, get used to turning. Even with ballast, you'll need to lean your weight into the turn to keep the sidecar on the road."

Ray glanced over at Grace. Her skin had gone a sickly shade of gray and she gripped the edge of the sidecar with a look of determination.

What the hell have I gotten us into?

"Hang on," he said, attempting to make light of the situation.

Benny's arms tightened.

"Not that hard, son."

"Sorry."

The band around his waist relaxed and Ray eased out on the clutch, accelerated through the shimmy, maneuvered the first right turn okay and then a left. Over-confident, he took the next right too sharp and fast. The sidecar lifted and headed for a power pole. Grace screamed. Benny screamed. Ray was too busy getting the bike under control to scream, but he wanted to.

He got them stopped and they sat for a few seconds with the bike half up on the sidewalk, its engine lobbing patiently, the nose of the sidecar inches from the pole.

Finally Grace asked, "Do you know what you did wrong?"

"Yep."

"Good." She released her grip on the sidecar and folded her hands in her lap, looking for all the world like somebody's grandma out for a relaxing Sunday afternoon drive. "Then let's be goin' to Vegas."

~~~

The sky over Albuquerque burned red as dusk settled in. While Benny and Grace rested in their rooms, Ray began packing the saddlebags and the sidecar's storage compartment. He tied the tent to the backrest. Benny's cowboy hat would have to stay behind. When Ray suggested the same for the pirate hat, Benny put up such a fuss that Ray relented and found a way to secure it to the Harley's windshield just above the headlamp.

The Black Pearl. It had a nice ring to it. And now it was dressed the part. Ray put what remained of the money in a small leather bag and strapped it to the handlebars where he could keep an eye on it. He knew Johnny would eventually catch up with them. It was just a matter of where and when. He hoped he had a plan by then. He asked Grace to trust him, but he wasn't sure he trusted himself. What kind of man spent money that didn't belong to him on a full-dress Harley Davidson with sidecar? But damn, it felt right.

He'd never ridden in a sidecar before and decided to see how it fit.

~~~

"The search has been called off for Grace Brown, reported missing since Sunday. Mrs. Brown's husband, Reverend Edward Brown, heard from his wife in a phone call made by her late this afternoon. Reverend Brown didn't want to go on camera, but issued a statement thanking everyone involved in the search, and apologized for causing undue concern. He wouldn't say where his wife called from, only that she sounded well and knew where she was, discounting earlier fears that Mrs. Brown may have been suffering from memory loss and had become disoriented. Grace Brown's disappearance coincided with the theft of Arleeta Collins's car, a blue Honda, from the United Christian Methodist parking lot. Mrs. Collins, you may recall, is Reverend Brown's sister. The car was later found abandoned on Interstate 40. Mr. Brown confirmed that his wife borrowed the car without his sister's knowledge – "

Grace turned off the motel room's TV. *Lord have mercy, now the whole congregation thinks I'm a car thief, on top of everything else.* She could see Gladys Turner's pitched mouth and Elsie Boucher shaking her head in disapproval. Busybodies, the both of them.

But what troubled Grace most was that Ed told the police she suffered from memory loss. *May have become disoriented.* All the times he let on like her forgetfulness weren't nothing, dismissed her fears and made her feel foolish for worrying, he'd been pretending. Why?

The answer came at her broadside. Denial. *I did the same thing to Papa when his mind began to slip. I tried to protect him. I covered for him, pretended he was all right, hoping to make it true.* It tore her inside-out to see her papa, the man she looked up to, cherished and drew strength from, deteriorate before her eyes.

Eddy told her more than once she was his rock, how he couldn't do the things Jesus expected of him without her by his side. How would he cope if something happened to her?

"Oh, Eddy, I've been so blind."

Grace sat on the edge of the bed and thanked the Lord for opening her eyes. She asked Him to forgive her shortsightedness. She prayed for guidance in purging her self-centered ways. She thanked Him for her loving husband's devotion and prayed for the chance to make things right at home. *And please, Lord, if it be your will, no more break-downs or kidnappings or shooting. These things I pray in Jesus' name, amen.*

Grace felt lighter for having her burden lifted. She went out to let Ray know the police weren't looking for her anymore.

She found him reclined in the sidecar, legs up, head tipped back, staring at the night sky. He made getting comfortable in the casket-shaped appendage look easier than she knew it to be. A body should have more than a few inches between the road and their backside. And if mechanic Andy hadn't been there to catch her when she tried to climb out the first time, she would have tumbled onto her head. She weren't ungrateful, but riding in a sidecar would take some gettin' used to.

After giving Ray the news update, she asked, "Still can't sleep?"

"Last time I fell asleep, my son almost drowned." He drew in a breath full of weariness. "Time before that, my wife died."

Grace didn't know what to say that wouldn't sound trite or condescending, so she let it be. "Mind if I have a sit-down?"

He patted the Harley's broad, curved seat. She stepped onto the chrome floorboard and hefted herself up. The seat cupped her bottom like a padded saddle. "I'll trade you," she said.

Ray gave a commiserating smile. "Ever driven a motorcycle?"

"Never been on one 'til now." She grasped the handlebar grips and leaned forward, pretending to race into the wind. "How do I look?"

"Like Marlon Brando."

"Hah." Grace sat up. "Think we're doing the right thing?"

"Probably not. Don't seem to be any turning back, though."

Then he told her about the plans he and Virginia made, and Grace understood why he spent Johnny's money.

"She talked to me," Ray said, "back in Santa Fe." He looked at her like he expected her to scoff at him. "That's how I knew Benny was in the pool."

Grace nodded. "Her spirit rides with you."

"I'd rather have her." His admission broke

Grace's heart. He drew his gaze back up to the stars and asked, "How do you do it? How do you get over losing the people you love?"

"Faith."

Ray shook his head. "I don't believe in a god that would let people die before their time. Gin was only fifty-seven."

Grace acknowledged his feelings. "I was fifteen when they told us my brother Joe had been killed in Korea." She could still see the will to live drain from Papa's body at the news. "Grandma James wanted me to go to church with her and pray for Joe's soul. I told her I wasn't prayin' to no god that would take my brother from me. I told her I hated God."

"What did she do?"

"Slapped my sassy mouth. She never struck me before. It scared me so bad, I went to church with her."

"Did it help?"

"No, sir. I sat in that pew with a sour face the whole time, hating God for pilin' more misery on me. It wasn't until years later, after Papa died and I met Ed, I figured it out. God never promised life would be fair. But He does promise that when we're confronted with hardship, we'll find the strength to endure, long as we have faith."

Ray seemed to give her words some thought before stating, "The only thing I have faith in is that boy." He pointed his chin at the hotel room door where Benny lay sleeping.

Ed might have tried to change his mind, convince him to let God in. But that was Ed's way, not hers. Grace knew by the look on Ray's face he would reject anything that smacked of preaching. Just as she and Papa did at Joe's death.

It wasn't Ray's faith in God that needed worked on. Grief had robbed him of faith in himself.

17: Let's Ride

Dawn wouldn't arrive for another hour, but once Benny got up, Ray didn't see any reason to wait. They crammed their belongings into every compartment and nook of the Harley and sidecar, donned their new leathers and boots and helmets, and saddled up. Ray hoped his son would relax enough to ease up on his gorilla hold once they'd been on the road a bit. But for now, he found the closeness a comfort.

Before leaving Albuquerque, he drove them by Andy's shop for one more look at the Olds. It sat inside a six-foot-high chain-link fence, under the beam of a streetlight. Burgundy and chrome representing thirty-eight years of memories. He told Grace it was just a car, but it felt like a chunk of his soul sitting there, abandoned. The 442 had been his salvation when his tour in Vietnam ended, the miles he put on the open road his sanity. When life didn't make sense, pushed too hard, he drove.

Just like he did now, he realized.

"'kay, Dad," Benny said over his shoulder. The boy lowered his voice and did his Schwarzenegger impression. "We'll be bock."

Ray paid Andy in advance for the repairs to the Olds, took one of the shop's cards so he could call in a couple weeks, all on the assumption they'd "be bock," as Benny put it. But doubt gnawed at him. The same doubt he experienced watching their Ohio home recede in the rearview mirror. Would he ever see house or car again?

Ray patted his son's gloved hands linked at his stomach. He couldn't do any more than that without losing to the lump in his throat.

~~~

Dawn broke behind a bank of low, dark clouds. As they crossed the Continental Divide, elevation 7,275 feet, it began to rain. It rained so hard, Ray couldn't see more than a few feet in front of the bike, its headlamp useless at cutting through the torrent.

"Stop, Dad!"

Ray didn't want to. He hoped to ride through it. But the farther they went, the worse it got, like a cow pissin' on a flat rock. Drops so fat they soaked through the seams of his leathers. Cold needles coursed off his helmet and found the opening of his jacket collar, ran down his back and soaked his t-shirt and underwear. He glanced over at Grace. She looked as miserable as he felt, her shoulders hunched against the onslaught.

Ray pulled to the side of the road.

Benny pushed at him to get off the bike. "The tent!" he yelled.

Of course.

~~~

Grace smiled at the sight they made, the three of them huddled beside the Interstate again, using the open tent as a tarp against the weather. She had to wonder how the boy knew they would need it. Raindrops pelted the treated nylon like steel BBs. The Black Pearl, as Benny and Ray come to call it, sat a few feet away, at the mercy of God's will. Fat drops bounced off the tank, pooled in the seat, cascaded from the saddlebags. Ray braved the onslaught extra minutes to snap the cover on the sidecar and keep it from becoming a bathtub. The rain fell hard and straight, pulling the temperature down with it. Grace shivered and Ray put his free arm around her shoulders. Benny hugged her from the other side. Their caring lodged in her heart like a warm ember.

"Sure is nice we have this tent to take cover under," she commented, her voice the only dry thing for miles.

She felt Ray's laughter vibrate up through him. "Sure is."

~~~

It made Benny happy that Daddy wasn't mad about the tent anymore. He didn't know who told him to take it. Sometimes he heard a voice that almost sounded like Mama talking to him. But it couldn't be Mama. Not when he made her cry and she died.

He didn't tell Daddy he had another nightmare back at the motel. His face hurt when he woke up. Daddy came in to say it was time to go and saw him splashing cold water on his cheeks. Benny said nothing was wrong. Daddy just told him to get his things together and bring them out to the bike, but Benny saw his sad face. Benny guessed maybe his dad could hear people's thoughts sometimes too, because he always knew when he was being lied to.

~~~

Minutes later the sun broke through the

clouds and the flat-topped butte in the distance glowed yellow and salmon. Grace breathed deep of the rain-washed air as she watched her soggy companions attempt to fold the tent and get it back into its bag. Her brain felt as sharp as the sun's reflection in the motorcycle's wet chrome.

"You could help, 'stead of standin' there grinning," Ray grumbled, then winked at her.

Grace's grin broadened. "You boys are doing a fine job without me gettin' in the way."

"Yeah," Benny sighed.

The boy could say a mouthful with that one word. This time it carried a load of frustration. The six-sided floor of the tent resisted being folded into a square. It flung water in their faces as they wrestled it into shape. Once they managed to get the dripping nylon folded and rolled, they struggled to shove it back into a bag that appeared to have shrunk.

Yes, Grace could have helped. And she would have done a better job of it. Her papa used to brag on how she could get ten pounds of shit in a five pound bag. But she enjoyed watching father and son work it out between them.

"It's not pretty," Ray stated, strapping the lumpy bag to the bike's backrest. "But it'll do."

"It'll do," Benny parroted, and gave the bag a couple pats of his own.

Grace headed for the sidecar. "Then let's go find us a dry place to eat and warm up."

~~~

That place turned out to be a McDonald's in Gallup. Ray had to admit, for a fast-food joint, the coffee tasted mighty good, the breakfast sandwich so-so but filling. In the half hour it took to get there, the sun had already begun to dry things out, including them.

"I figure between our body heat and the day's heat, we'll be dry before lunch," he said.

Grace and Benny nodded and continued eating.

The dressing on his shoulder wound needed changed. They pulled into a gas station and convenience store on the way out of town. While Ray filled the bike, Grace and Benny bought another tube of antibacterial cream and a roll of gauze to restock the first-aid kit. Ray moved the bike to a patch of sun at the end of the parking lot, pulled off his jacket and t-shirt, and let Grace bandage him. Benny scrambled onto the bike's seat and leaned in for a closer look.

"Sorry, Dad."

"It's okay, son. My butt hurts worse."

Benny snickered and Grace joined him with one of those half-there responses that had Ray looking at her.

"You can put your shirt on," she told him.

He did, then shrugged into his leather jacket and asked, "Ready to ride?"

Benny piped in. "Yeah, Dad."

Grace stowed the first-aid kit. Her hands stilled on the saddlebag flap as she gazed northwest.

To nothing in particular, that Ray could see. "What's up, Grace?"

"Can't exactly say," she answered, her voice almost a whisper. Then she seemed to shake herself out of it and reached for her helmet. "I'm ready."

~~~

Twenty miles later, they crossed into Arizona. An hour after that, Ray's tailbone throbbed like a toothache and a gas pain cramped his gut. He stood on the Harley's floorboards to take the pressure off, but that put his ass in Benny's face.

"Da-a-ad!"

Ray waggled his hips to tease the boy. Benny slapped him on the butt. Leather met leather with a *thwack* loud enough to hear over the rumble of the bike. Ray didn't know if it was the slap or the hip waggle, but the gas bubble broke loose and he ripped an uncontrollable fart – also loud enough to hear over the bike.

"Oh man!" Benny gagged and waved his arms.

Ray's face grew hot in spite of the air hitting him at seventy miles an hour over the windshield. He glanced at Grace. She had her face turned away, as though interested in the passing scenery. But her shaking shoulders didn't leave any doubt in Ray's mind that she heard and was trying not to let him see her laugh. He eased his aching tailbone back onto the seat. Before he could recover from his embarrassment and apologize, Grace pointed at a sign to the Petrified Forest National Park coming up on their right.

"Let's stop and stretch!" she shouted.

Ray took the exit. He had just about decided not to make any mention of his embarrassing body function, but when he parked in front of the Visitors Center and swung off the bike, another fart ripped loose.

"Lord have mercy," Grace exclaimed. "No more breakfast sandwiches for you!"

"Amen to that."

~~~

From the picnic area at the Chinde Point overlook, the northernmost of eight stops on the scenic loop, Grace took in the eroded hills of sandstone and clay that gave the Painted Desert its name. Horizontal bands of red and orange and ivory reminded her of the quilt Grandma James made from old neckties decades ago.

Ray moved up to stand next to her. She could tell by the way he didn't quite hold himself straight his tailbone bothered him. She could say the same about her own backside after a few miles in that sidecar. Behind them, Benny fished through the saddlebags and mumbled something about his camera.

"Mighty pretty country," Ray said.

She pointed north. "Over that way's the Navajo Nation, and in the middle of it is the Hopi Reservation. Papa took me and brother Joe through there when I was fourteen." Recollection of the trip came on her slow, beginning back in Gallup, more a feeling than something concrete she could identify. Standing here now, she remembered like it happened yesterday. "We didn't know at the time, but it was the last trip we'd be making with Joe 'fore he got drafted."

Ray didn't say anything, just nodded.

"Papa's mother, my Grandma James, was half Cherokee," Grace went on. "Papa used to say that's where he got his wanderin' feet, even though Grandma James reminded him, time and time again, Cherokees weren't nomads."

"And your mother?"

Grace sucked her teeth. "She left when I was about eleven, got tired of moving around all the time, wanted to settle down, but that wasn't Papa's way. She wanted to take me with her, but that weren't *my* way. And Joe...well, he and Mother never did get along." She could still hear their heated scenes, yelling punctuated by the slam of a door as one of them, usually Joe, stormed out. It only happened when Papa was away, sitting at a poker table somewhere. But he must have known, because he started taking her and Joe with him the older they got.

"Did you ever see her again?"

"On birthdays and Christmases, when she could find us. She'd send us things. Then Papa got a call that she remarried and was living in Florida." That was the last time any of them heard from her until Joe's funeral. She showed up in a mink wrap and leopard sling-back pumps. All Papa had to say was it appeared she finally found her high cotton. The memory still had the power to poke at a sore spot in Grace. She looked up at Ray. "What about your folks?"

"They're both gone. They owned a hardware store in Sandy, Oregon. My brother, Frank, still lives there with his wife. They took up running the business when Mom and Dad decided to retire."

"Did you come up in one place your whole childhood?"

"I did."

"You got you some deep down roots then. Papa used to tell me, 'Baby girl, remember where you come from.' I done me a mess of moving and seeing in my years, but my roots will always be in a little piece of land Grandma and Grandpa James owned north of Altheimer, Arkansas. That's where my world began."

"Guess I never looked at it that way. When you're nineteen and things are heating up in Vietnam and Uncle Sam calls, a little place like Sandy, Oregon, seems unimportant."

"But you miss it."

Ray shot her a quick look, as if her observation caught him by surprise. "I didn't realize how much 'til I started heading west. Now the closer I get, the closer I wanna be."

"When was the last time you went home?"

He thought on it a second. "Ten years ago."

~~~

June, 1997. Frank called to let him know their mom had died of a stroke. Nobody knew she had any health issues, outside of a little arthritis, even her doctor, so the news hit hard. August of the same year, Ray flew to Portland a second time, for their dad's service. Died of loneliness, people said. This time no one was much surprised. Losing his wife after fifty-six years of marriage stole Dad's will to live. Ray took Karen with him both trips, but Virginia stayed home with Benny. She didn't want to travel with a one-year-old still in diapers.

Ray thought he better understood Grace's need to reconnect with her past. He missed his folks and the town he grew up in. He missed Frank and Babs. Talking about them intensified the missing.

It struck him that Virginia died in June, like his mom ten years ago. Now it was August, the month Dad died. *I need to call my daughter*.

~~~

Grace looked at the map and said the road they were on looped south through the Petrified Forest and would take them back to I-40 farther west, to a place called Holbrook.

Benny took pictures of teepees made of

sandstone, and a bridge of agates, But he didn't see any forest. When Daddy needed to stretch again, they stopped at the Rainbow Forest Museum and watched a short movie about how there was a flood years and years ago, when dinosaurs still lived, and the trees got buried for a long time and turned into stone. After the movie, Grace wanted to walk the Giant Logs trail behind the museum. Benny took pictures of the pretty wood-shaped rocks that looked like tree trunks.

And he took pictures of his dad and Grace standing together talking. In a few days Grace would go back home and it would be a long time before they'd all be together again. He wanted lots of pictures to help him remember.

~~~

Ray stopped in Holbrook to call Karen. The goobers took turns saying hi to their grandpa, then argued about something in the background while their mommy talked over them. Ray smiled at the feeling of normalcy their voices carried across the miles.

"I've been so worried, Daddy. You guys have been gone five days. Are you okay?"

"We're fine as frog's hair," Ray replied. "We're a stone's throw from the Grand Canyon."

"So you could be home next week?"

Ray hesitated. Next week sounded too soon. "I can't say for sure. There's still time before Benny has to be back in school. We just might find something else we need to see." Like Las Vegas. "I'll give you a call in a few days and let you know."

"How is that smarty pants brother of mine?"

Ray heard the forced cheeriness in her voice. Unhappy with his answer, she nevertheless let it go for now. He appreciated that. "I'll let him tell you his own self," Ray said. "I love you, pumpkin."

"I love you too, Daddy."

It didn't occur to Ray, until the receiver was in his son's hand, Benny might spill the beans about Grace, the bag of money, shooting at Johnny, almost drowning, the Olds, the Harley.

"Keep it short, son."

Benny gave him *the look* – lips compressed, brows drawn low over his almond eyes, nostrils flaring with a forced sigh. But whether it meant "mind your own business" or "I'm not that stupid," Ray couldn't be sure.

The boy pressed the receiver to his ear and said, "Hi, honey." He turned away so Ray couldn't see his face. Ray stood poised, ready to grab the receiver back and cut the conversation short if need be.

"Yeah." ... "Good." ... "Yeah." ... "Love you too." ... "'kay. Bye."

Benny hung up and looked at Ray with a maturity that left him speechless. "Let's ride," his son said, and took his hand.

18: Catch-up

On Route 66, at Second Street and Kinsley Avenue in downtown Winslow, Arizona, a bronze statue of a man in jeans and vest, his guitar propped on the toe of one boot, stands next to a lamppost. A woman with long, blonde hair sits at the wheel of a red, flatbed Ford, watching from a mural on the wall behind him. A Bald Eagle perches on the window ledge above.

Standin' on the Corner Park, inspired by The Eagles hit "Take it Easy," was no more than that, a street corner, but the song had been a favorite of Gin's, so Ray went out of his way to stop.

Grace took a picture of him and Benny standing on each side of the bronze musician. Benny pretended to strum the guitar and rock out. Ray smiled, though the emotion fell short of his heart. He wanted Gin to be there, to share the moment with them. Things were changing too fast and he had no control over any of it. The feeling they'd never be here again, like the song said, weighed heavy on him.

"Ray?"

He shoved his hands into the pockets of his jacket and looked at Grace standing beside him, unable to speak around the lump in his throat.

"How many women you got on your mind?" she asked softly.

He swallowed the lump and quoted a line from the song. "'One says she's a friend of mine.'"

"Don't never forget it."

Ray saw the compassion on her face and nodded. Regardless of where they might be a week from now, a year from now, this woman would always be his friend.

On the tail of that realization came another. "You know, if we drive straight through, we can be in Vegas tonight."

~~~

We can be in Vegas tonight. Grace's skin danced. "Let's ride."

~~~

Benny felt different. Good different. He remembered when Thelma said something crossed over in her. That's how he felt. He noticed it when he talked to Karen. When Dad handed him the phone, he knew his sister wouldn't understand about everything that happened since they left. She talked to him like he was still a little boy. He missed her a lot, but she didn't know him anymore.

He leaned against the backrest of the Black Pearl and tipped his head up. The air smelled magic. It brushed his face like Mama's warm touch. Her closeness tingled inside him.

He looked over at Grace in the sidecar. Her color halo shined brighter than he ever saw it before, even with her helmet on. She stared at the trees zooming by like she didn't really see them, and Benny wondered if she might be thinking about her papa.

~~~

A sleeveless, psychedelic palazzo pantsuit of orange, brown and yellow on a black background, a v-neck collar with wide lapels, and orange buttons the size of half dollars. She had her hair done up in a Jackie Kennedy-style bouffant.

The memory came at Grace unexpected and

strong. Papa hadn't been the only one making a fashion statement that day at the Stardust. She all but forgot about that pantsuit and impossible hairdo. But the air vibrated here. Conducted energy. The closer she got to Vegas, the more she felt the memories current through her.

~~~

Ray cruised, lost in the hypnotic rumble of the bike between his legs. He drove past one Flagstaff exit after another. They wouldn't need to stop for gas or food until Kingman. He drove into the afternoon sun, his dark glasses shielding his eyes as the Interstate cut through stands of tall pines.

The air smelled of Christmas trees. A smell Ray used to enjoy. Now he wondered how he could survive the holidays without Gin. She took care of the shopping and baking and organizing. She filled the house with cheer. He never thought about it coming to an end. He never thought she would go first. It should have been him. Gin was the strong one. She could have handled life without him, made a better job of it than he was doing.

Ray honey, you need to wake up now.

"Why?" he asked, too low for anybody but himself to hear. It took a couple more seconds to bring his brain into focus, realize where he was and that his dead wife sent him another warning. He caught a flash of headlights in the right side-mirror. A silver car behind them, lights on, off, on, signaling as it closed in on them fast.

Three things went through Ray's mind: the Olds sitting under the streetlight where anybody from the main road could see it; he didn't tell Andy the mechanic to keep his mouth shut about the Harley; and with the sidecar, there wasn't much chance of the bike outrunning whoever followed them.

It must be Johnny. Ray knew the asshole would catch up with them sooner or later, but he had hoped for later, had hoped to make Vegas first. With no clue how to explain spending the guy's money, Ray signaled, intending to pull over and give it his best shot.

The right side-mirror exploded.

~~~

Grace scowled at the shards of glass in her lap, heard a soft pop and looked up at the hole punched in the mirror's chrome frame. *Why, that looks like –*

"Hang on!" Ray shouted and accelerated. "The asshole's shooting at us!"

"Johnny?" Grace twisted around and saw

the small silver car closing in on them, the driver's left arm thrust out the window as if pointing at them. The arm jerked and Grace felt something rush past her cheek. *Pop!*

"Lord have mercy!" she squeaked and jerked forward.

Ray took an unimproved road off the Interstate so fast the sidecar became airborne. An instant later it landed hard and knocked the wind from her. She held on and prayed.

Lord Jesus in heaven, watch over us in our hour of need. Protect us from our transgressor, may his aim be lousy. Amen.

She looked over at Benny clutching his daddy, eyes shut tight, and a chill flushed through her. The child may as well have a target painted on the back of his jacket. She released her seatbelt and scrambled to her knees on the sidecar's seat, intent on pulling him in with her, use herself as a shield. She reached out and Ray took another sharp turn. The sidecar lifted and the sleeping bag she'd been using for extra padding slid beneath her knees.

When the sidecar made its hard landing, Grace shot back and out like a cork from a champagne bottle. She closed her eyes, pulled into a ball and hit the ground rolling.

~~~

The Black Pearl hit a hole and Benny bounced up and banged his helmet against his dad's. He wanted to yell at Daddy to slow down, but if they did, the bad man would catch them. He wished he had Daddy's gun so he could shoot back, but that was a dumb idea, because the gun didn't have any bullets. And he couldn't let go of his dad or he might fall off. They hit another hole and he bit his tongue. It hurt and made his eyes water. He looked over to see if Grace was okay. The sidecar was empty and he screamed.

~~~

My boy's shot!

Ray hit the brakes, front and back, and the Harley fishtailed to a stop. He scrambled off the bike, pulling Benny with him, and started patting the boy down. "Where'd he get you, son? Where ya hit?"

Benny swatted his hands away. "Grace is gone!"

Ray stared at the empty sidecar in disbelief. "Where the hell did she go?"

"I don't know," Benny cried.

Ray looked back the way they had come. He took the turn-off thinking it might be a service road, hoping it wasn't road enough for Johnny

223

to follow. A few yards in, the so-called service road petered into a dry wash even the cumbersome Harley had a hard time managing. With all the bouncing and bone-jarring, he hadn't noticed the weight change when he lost his ballast. How far back did he lose her? Surrounded by a whole lot of desert rock and scrub brush, he saw no sign of Grace. His stomach sank.

A glint of silver caught his eye. Johnny's car jumped and staggered over ruts and potholes too fast, headed their way. Grace would have to wait. "Get on the bike," Ray said.

"Oh, man!" Benny pointed at the flat rear tire.

"Shit!" Ray looked back at the car getting closer. Pushing Benny toward a pile of rocks, he yelled, "Hide!" and watched long enough to make sure his son did as told. Then he unbuckled the bag from the bike's handlebar, shouted, "I'll be back," and ran.

19: Bird Lady

Grace scrambled to the top of the embankment she had tumbled over and removed her helmet. The canyon extended forever in all directions, sandstone formations in vivid shades of rust and umber and fire, precarious spires at the mercy of erosion. Heat shimmered off the red dust and an untamed energy pulsed the air. It stirred the Cherokee blood that pumped through her veins. Standing in this rugged place made the sweet ache of missing Papa and brother Joe palpable.

The high desert sky stretched as wide and endless as the canyon, an unchanging azure canopy. A lone Bald Eagle rode the thermals. She watched it tuck its wings and dive in the direction of a low dust cloud dissipating in the distance. *I need to find them boys.*

The sharp report of a gunshot echoed up the canyon. "Lord have mercy!" Grace yelped. Constricted by tight leathers and an ache in her backside, she made a hobbling run toward the sound.

She saw the motorcycle first, squatting on a flat rear tire, abandoned. Then she spotted Benny in his pirate hat, the motorcycle's saddlebags slung over his shoulders, picking his way around rocks and agave spines as though he had a destination in mind.

"Benjamin!" she shouted.

He stopped and looked off in the wrong direction because that's the way the sound carried. Grace waved her arms over her head. Benny circled round 'til he caught sight of her. He jumped and waved back, the saddlebags sliding off his shoulders. Grace drew in a breath of relief that the child appeared uninjured.

"Where you headed?" she called.

He pointed. Grace stared for several seconds before she saw the sod roof of a small, round dwelling.

"Bird lady!" Benny shouted.

"What about your daddy?" she asked, making her way toward him. "Where's Ray?"

"He's safe," Benny said. "Come," he took her

arm when she reached him, "the bird lady waits."

~~~

Ray sat up to a fresh stab of pain. He drew his jacket open and saw the blood on his t-shirt.

"Crap. I'm shot again."

He removed his helmet, shrugged out of his jacket and worked the t-shirt off. Using the shirt to dab at the wound, he saw the bullet had only grazed him. He gave a wry croak that scraped the back of his throat. *What are the odds of getting shot twice in less than a week and losing only a few layers of hide each time?*

He struggled to his feet. By tomorrow he knew his legs would remind him of his marathon dash. He rolled his t-shirt lengthwise and tied it around his waist to put pressure on the wound. Not pretty, but it would do for the time being. Then he shrugged back into his leather jacket and picked up his helmet. A high-pitched *kleek-ik-ik-ik* drew his gaze skyward. He saw the white head and tail of a Bald Eagle as its massive wingspan blocked the sun.

The eagle will guide you.

The thought entered Ray's head as clear as if somebody whispered in his ear, and he felt that tingle up his spine. He squinted against the afternoon heat shimmering off the semi-arid landscape. Benny is with the bike, he assured himself.

Where you should be.

Looking back along the dry wash, Ray saw a glint of chrome. He drew up straight and pressed his hand to the pain in his side. He found his sunglasses crushed in the middle of a tire track, gave the area a quick scan for the handlebar bag. It most likely landed in the open and Johnny now had it. But Ray didn't want to take the chance that it lay in a bush or behind a rock and Johnny was doubling back to take more potshots at him. Being shot and used as a car hurdle wasn't exactly how Ray envisioned their exchange going, but if the asshole had the bag, it might buy them time to make some sort of plan.

After a few minutes of searching and coming up empty-handed, Ray headed back to the bike. His gunshot wound throbbed with the rhythm of his heartbeat and his over-worked leg muscles began to seize up on him. For long, painful minutes, the glint of the bike in the distance didn't seem to get any closer. Heat radiated from the desert floor and dragged at his boots. By the time he reached the Harley, the lightheadedness of exhaustion made the ground swim.

Something's not right, he thought. He blinked several times, trying to bring his gritty eyes and fuzzy brain into focus. Then, "That asshole son-of-a-bitch took our gear. Of all the low down – "

Where's Benny?

Ray looked to the rock pile where he told the boy to hide. "Son, you can come out now!"

His arid voice ricocheted back at him, followed by silence. Pushing against a surge of adrenaline, Ray circled the rocks. A striped whiptail switched and skittered away. No Benny. Ray's sweat-drenched skin went cold.

"Benny! Where are you?" Desperate to control the growing panic in his voice, he forced a halfhearted laugh. "You goin' pee again?"

He listened for any sound of his son. The hammer of his own pulse dulled his perception. The desert's calm taunted.

"Damn it, Ben, answer me!"

But the only answer he got was a haunting cackle from the eagle soaring overhead.

The last of Ray's strength drained from his limbs. He leaned against the rocks to keep from collapsing. The fear of not measuring up, of making the wrong decisions, of not protecting his son, ran unchecked down his face. Hot, blistering tears too long held in. He made one stupid mistake after another on this trip, like it was some kind of game. How could he have let it get so out of control? The thought of somebody hurting his son pierced his heart like jagged ice.

And where was Grace? Did he leave her lying in a ditch someplace with a broken neck? Or shot and bleeding out? He needed to go look for her. He needed to find his son. Swiping at his face, Ray pushed away from the rocks and collapsed to his knees, his legs gone.

Impotent rage consumed him. "God damn it!" he bellowed and threw his helmet across the desert. The helmet careened off a rock formation ten feet away and came to rest in a low juniper. Ray stared at it, unable to move or think, his body spent, his brain shut down.

How long he stared before noticing the shadow flash over his helmet, he couldn't say. There it was again. And again. He blinked and looked at the eagle circling above. Foreboding slithered up Ray's back, cold and wet. *Do Bald Eagles circle carrion – like little boys and elderly women – the way vultures do?*

The bird tipped its wings and flew

northward. Ray watched its flight and saw it pass over an earthen roof in the distance.

~~~

The low, six-sided dwelling of rough logs pushed up from the desert floor. Hunkered in a natural bowl formed by the rocks surrounding it, Ray doubted he would have seen it if not for the eagle. As he approached the wood-slab door, he imagined a weathered hermit answering, a recluse with yellowed teeth and rheumy eyes.

Before he had a chance to knock, the door opened. Ray stared stupidly at the striking Indian woman in a sleeveless turquoise dress, her smooth black hair falling to a small waist. She regarded him with eyes so big and dark a man could wander for days in them.

"Hello, Ray."

"How – "

Those dark eyes shined above even white teeth. "You may call me Rose."

"Hi, Rose. How – "

She gave a dry laugh. "We don't say 'how' anymore, *bilagáana*." The draft from the door as she stepped back and pulled it wide caught her skirt, causing the crimson and green band at the hem to float then settle mid-calf. She had the daintiest feet Ray had ever seen, encased in suede mocs with a beaded eagle on each toe.

"They've been waiting for you," she said.

Ray looked up. "They?" He squinted past her, his eyes not yet adjusted to the cool, dim room.

Two small windows on opposing walls provided the only light. He made out a potbelly stove in the center, a hand pump at the sink against the back wall, and the silhouettes of two people sitting at a table off to the side. He recognized the outline of Grace's frizzed hair. The squat shape next to her raised a hand in greeting.

"Benny?" Two strides propelled Ray inside. He pulled his son out of the chair and into his arms. "God, I thought – " He stopped, unable to voice what he thought without breaking down again. He pressed the boy to him, felt the warmth of his body, smelled his hair.

Benny mumbled, "Can't breathe, Dad."

Ray pulled back and held his son at arm's length. "Why didn't you stay put?" he demanded. "You scared the hell outta me."

Instead of an apology, Benny looked over at Rose still standing by the door, something close to reverence in his eyes. "She called me."

"Called you?" Ray caught himself short of asking "how" again. He already had his answer anyway. The eagle. Rose sent the bird to guide them all here.

Ray couldn't wrap his brain around that idea – the unreality of the situation they were in, the impossibility of finding an Indian woman living out here in the middle of nowhere – so he didn't try. He released his son and looked at Grace. "Are you okay?"

She tsked. "Outside of a bruised behind, I be fine."

"I'm sorry I didn't come back for you."

"Hush that." She gave a dismissive wave, then asked, "Have you been shot again?"

"I'm beginning to feel like a target."

Rose closed the door and crossed to a cabinet of open shelves next to the sink, her movements as easy as a stream coursing around smooth stones. Sage and rosemary toyed with Ray's senses in her wake. She took down a small, hand-labeled jar, pumped water onto a washcloth and turned to him.

"Let me dress that."

A self-conscious second ticked through him, a hesitation that took him by surprise. He looked from the damp cloth in her hand to her unreadable dark eyes. Annoyed with himself, he took his jacket off and hung it over the back of a chair, flinched at the touch of her cool fingers on his abdomen when she peeled his crude t-shirt bandage away and tossed it into the sink. She washed his wound, then daubed green salve on it. Ray couldn't read the label on the jar, figured it must be some secret Native concoction. It smelled like the desert. The pain in his side dulled almost immediately.

"Would you mind putting some of that up here?" he asked, indicating his shoulder wound.

Rose drew back the cotton gauze. "No need," she said. "It's already scabbing." She pressed the cover back into place. "You heal fast."

Ray grunted. "Guess I can do that much right at least."

Rose put the salve back on its shelf among other assorted jars, then pulled down a box of gauze and tape. "You should learn to duck," she said, and began covering the fresh wound.

"I'll take it into consideration."

Ray found the woman mesmerizing: the fall of her long hair over one shoulder, the brush of her fingers against his skin, the sough of her skirt on her bare legs when she shifted.

"That was Johnny chasing us, wasn't it," Grace said, breaking the spell.

Ray looked over at her. Now that his eyes

had adjusted to being inside, he could see the sooty cast of exhaustion on her face. A familiar regret tugged at him for getting her into this mess. "Yes. And it isn't going to take him long to discover his bag of money is short. We need to get back on the road ASAP."

"He won't find you here," Rose said, not looking up from her work.

Ray frowned at the top of her head. "We found you."

"Because you needed to."

And Johnny doesn't? The asshole had proven himself mighty damn capable of trailing them so far. "What're you going to do, put some kind of disappearing spell on the place?"

The rent of medical tape punctuated the silence that followed. Rose lifted her face and the shift in her dark eyes sent cool prickles dancing across Ray's skin. "Maybe I'm a little witchy-poo."

She held his gaze long enough to have him believing she could turn him into a toad on the spot, if she wanted to. Then she smiled and his breath stopped.

"You watch too many movies," she said, and finished dressing his wound.

"Dad?"

Again Ray found himself pulled from the

woman's disturbing ability to unsettle him. "What is it, son?"

The look on Benny's face drove all concerns of "witchy-poo" from Ray's thoughts. The boy reached inside his leather jacket and started drawing out bundles of money and laying them on the table.

"Aw hell."

"What's in the bag?" Grace asked, her voice a notch above a whisper.

"Dad's dirty underwear."

Ray stared at his son then the money, his exhausted brain unable to settle on a reaction.

"Sit down, Ray. Have a glass of cool water." Rose pushed him toward a chair.

Ray planted his feet. "Lady – "

"Rose."

"You don't get it, *Rose*. The guy who shot me isn't going be happy when he sees what's in that bag. He's armed and – "

"I told you he won't find this place."

"No offense, but I don't believe in spells and magic, witchy-poo or not."

"You've lost *hózhó*."

"What?"

"Harmony. Balance. *Diné* call it *hózhó*."

Ray didn't understand, nor did he care. "I haven't got time for this." He grabbed his jacket and turned toward the door. "I've got a tire to fix."

"Has she spoken to you?" Rose asked.

A shiver ran up Ray's spine and he stopped. He caught Benny's open-mouth stare as he turned to look at the woman.

She must have seen the truth in his eyes. "Many times, *aoó?*"

"Yes."

Benny gasped.

"Let her help you," Rose said.

"How?"

A brief smile touched her mouth. "Go for a walk." She pointed her chin toward the door.

"A walk?" Ray glanced at the door, then back at her and frowned. "I've been run down and shot by a man who wants his money back, my bike's got a flat, and you want me take a walk in the desert."

The woman held his gaze without speaking.

He shifted, felt naked under her stare. True, he hadn't put his jacket on yet – in fact, somewhere in the space between "got a tire to fix" and "walk in the desert," the jacket had slipped from his hand and lay at his feet – so, technically, he was naked from the waist up.

But this was a different kind of naked. He felt exposed and he didn't like it. "I need a shirt," he said, his tone abrupt.

Benny reached into one of the saddlebags and pulled out the Aunt Georgie shirt. It had been washed, along with everything else the boy puked on back in Oklahoma. The ugly fabric showed a galling resistance to wrinkles; the shirt sagged on Ray like a muumuu.

"Nice, Dad."

He felt ridiculous, but it beat standing bare to Rose's scrutiny. "Thanks, son." He swept his jacket up off the floor. "I've gotta go. It'll be dark soon."

"The dark isn't what you're afraid of," Rose said.

He gave her a sharp look. "I'm not afraid."

"When was the last time you slept?" she asked.

When my son almost drowned. "I don't know."

"Why?"

Her question confused him. Why didn't he know? Or why did he lie to her? "It's none of your business."

Again Rose held his look. The room seemed to fade as her eyes sucked him in. He thought of the eagle staring down at him, thought he heard its coarse laughter in his head.

He *was* afraid. Afraid to sleep. Afraid of what might be waiting for him in the desert.

Afraid to let his dead wife help him, whatever the hell that meant.

"Go," Rose said. "You'll know when it's time to return."

He looked over at Benny and Grace.

"'kay, Dad."

"We'll be fine," Grace told him.

Yes, they would. Whether he wanted to believe Rose or not – that Johnny wouldn't find them here – he trusted Grace to keep his boy safe until he returned with the Harley. Rose didn't need to know where he intended to head once he was out the door.

His throat clicked with a dry swallow. "What about water?" he asked.

"The desert will give you what you need," Rose said.

Ray pictured himself sucking on a cactus. Grace handed him a glass of water. It went down cool and fine. She refilled the glass and he drained it a second time.

Rose shoved him toward the door. "Go."

20: Taking a Walk

Grace watched the door close behind Ray. The poor man was so tired his backside left a third trail. Once again she prayed to Jesus to look after him. "What's going to happen out there?" she asked Rose.

Rose shrugged, said, "That's up to Ray," and turned to Benny. "You've had a long day, young man. Why don't you rest on the cot over here while your friend and I talk?"

"Yeah."

Benny lumbered to his feet, leaned in and gave Grace a peck on the cheek. "'G'night, honey." The child's gesture went straight to her heart and teared her eyes.

"Good night, sugar."

Rose helped him remove his jacket, boots and socks. He stretched out on the cot against the opposite wall and Rose pulled a handsome blanket of reds and browns and turquoise over him. Grace found herself wishing she could join him. Her body ached from one end to the other.

The bird lady, as Benny called her, was Navajo, but to Grace's knowing, they weren't on the reservation, which made her presence a curiosity. Grace respected the woman's right to reveal only what she chose. Still, when she returned to the table, Grace felt compelled to ask, "How did you know Ray's wife spoke to him?"

"I didn't. But the boy thought it might be so." Rose replenished their water. "His mind is clear."

"Yes."

"Most people fill their heads with too much noise."

A twinge of panic skittered through Grace. "That be so, but when the noise begins to fade..."

Rose waited, as if giving her time to finish the thought. But fear held Grace's tongue.

"You worry too hard on it," Rose said. "I know what you need." She went to the cabinet and pulled down a large towel, a flashlight and a tight bundle of herbs Grace took to be a smudge. "Get yourself a change of clothes and come with me."

Grace glanced over at Benny. He looked asleep already. "Where are we going?"

"Not far."

~~~

The claw-foot tub sat at the edge of a pool fed by hot springs spilling from the rocks above. Steam rose off the water in defiance of the desert heat. Juniper and Blackbrush crowded close, offering seclusion.

"Lord have mercy," Grace breathed.

"My old boyfriend and his buddies dragged the tub up here last summer, thinking it would impress me."

"Did it?"

Rose angled her a sly look. "For a time."

Their laughter filled the waning daylight. It felt good, two sisters sharing a bond. Grace felt the tension in her shoulders begin to ease. "Do you live here year round?"

"No. I teach fourth graders on the reservation during the school year. This is my summer resort." She said *summer resort* with a lah-dee-dah air that drew another laugh from Grace.

Rose piled the things she brought from the hogan onto the clothes in Grace's arms – capris, canvas shoes, her last clean blouse – and retrieved a section of plastic gutter tucked in the brush. She used the gutter as a flume to transfer hot mineral water from the falls into the tub. When the tub was full, she lit the fat, white candle sitting on a nearby rock and held the smudge in its flame until the herbs smoldered.

Grace recognized the smell of sage, a cleansing herb. When Papa took her and Joe to the Navajo Nation, they were invited to a storytelling circle. Everyone bathed in purifying sage smoke to drive out bad spirits that might try to influence the stories. The storytelling went long: *Diné* legends of Coyote, Spider Woman, Monster-Slayer. The experience taught Grace a deep respect for the spiritual traditions of her ancestors.

Rose coaxed the sage smoke over herself with a gentle sweep of her hand. She chanted soft words in her native tongue as she bathed her entire body, beginning at her feet and working upward in a figure-eight pattern. The hot springs splashed and played in the background. Grace watched the smoke climb and dissipate in the evening air.

"I release all negative energy," Rose finished, then motioned for Grace to step closer. "Allow the sacred smoke to cleanse your body and bring your spirit peace."

Grace stood quiet as Rose fanned the sage smoke over her. She closed her eyes and felt the Navajo woman's chants like balm on frayed nerves. She breathed deep, a lightheaded calm overtaking her.

"Let go of stagnant energy and allow light and love to protect you in the present," Rose said. She lingered a moment on Grace's heart area, then placed the smudge on the stone, next to the candle. "You have come a long way, my sister. Let the water heal you."

~~~

Ray walked into the setting sun. As he picked his way across the desert, the yellow-orange sky deepened to blood red then faded to muted pink, turning the surrounding rock formations into massive silhouettes against the horizon. He stopped for a few minutes to take it in.

"Man, that's pretty," he said to nobody but himself.

The evening air lost its fire, but the land continued to radiate heat. He glanced behind him for Rose's cabin but couldn't make it out. No glow of light in a window. No eagle circling over head.

He won't find this place.

Crap, Ray thought, I may not find it again either.

He walked on. Rocks cast long shadows in the growing darkness. Yucca spikes reached out and stabbed at his legs. He wished he had paid more attention to landmarks when he went through the area earlier, but other concerns occupied his mind at the time. Nothing looked familiar to his dog-tired brain.

What if he didn't return? What if he stumbled across a wild boar or cougar's den? Did they even have wild boar and cougar in this part of Arizona? It was a big country. What if he fell off a cliff or into a hole he couldn't see in the dark? He caught the toe of his boot on something that didn't give, lurched forward a couple steps before regaining his balance. A night creature skittered away, low and unseen, a few feet to his left. Ray's pulse skittered with it. He didn't need Rose to spook him; he was doing a fine job on his own.

The dark isn't what you're afraid of.

The beat of his erratic pulse settled as a sharp ache in his heart. He didn't want to face his fears. Not yet. *Where the hell is the bike?*

He stumbled over rocks and tangled with clumps of yucca awhile longer before admitting he didn't know which direction he should be headed. He wondered if the Indian woman had anything to do with his getting turned around, wanted to laugh at the thought but couldn't quite shake the suspicion.

Fatigue dragged at him. His boots felt like iron weights on his feet. Taking the next step became too much work. He resigned himself to the fact that he'd have to wait until daylight to find the Harley or the cabin. Maybe that's what Rose meant when she said he'd know when to return.

He found a low, flat rock to sit on. "Might as well get comfortable," he muttered, and proceeded to yank off his boots. "Go for a walk, she said. The desert will give you what you need, she said." The woman sure had a way of getting under a man's skin. He wrestled out of his sweaty socks and tucked them inside his boots. The night air felt good on his bare feet; soft dust sifted between his toes.

Gin liked to go barefoot. The memory broadsided him and honed the ache in his heart.

Let her help you.

She already has, Ray thought. If not for Gin, their son would have drowned. And if she hadn't warned him of Johnny's approach on the Interstate, all three of them could have been shot. What more was there?

Restless edginess made his skin itch. His clothes irritated and pulled. So he shed them – peeled his leather pants off, removed his briefs and his son's wild shirt, folded everything in a neat pile on the rock. It reminded him of a time when he was about ten. He and brother Frank and two other boys found a secluded swimming hole in an abandoned rock quarry. They dared each other to strip and jump in. Being the youngest and wanting to prove his manhood, Ray volunteered to go first. Summer hadn't heated up yet and the swimming hole lay in the shade of the Mount Hood National Forest. As soon as Ray's skinny body hit the frigid water, his manhood sucked up to nonexistence.

No danger of that here. Sunset had cooled the desert air, but it was far from uncomfortable, even to his scrawny bones. He'd always been lean. Gin used to tease him about it. She paraded around the house in a light cotton blouse and shorts – she may have thought her elbows ugly, but she'd been proud of her legs, and rightly so – while he wore rolled-up long sleeves and jeans.

Why did remembering something so simple

hurt so much?

Short on answers, he said, "I need to pee."

He walked up to a shoulder-high rock and pissed on its face free-hand. He always won the pissing contests he had with Frank and their swimming buddies, because he had the shortest name. It was legitimate too. His birth certificate said Ray, not Raymond like most people thought. And Frank was just Frank. Their folks believed in keeping things simple.

What the hell. He grabbed his dick and started writing but emptied his bladder before he made it to *y*. "You win," he told the desert.

The sky filled with sharp points of light. Millions of them. Ray picked a smooth spot in the dirt to sit cross-legged and stargaze. He had a 360-degree view of the show. The air smelled of sage and juniper and timelessness. The warm earth eased his tight legs and the dull throb of his tailbone. His hand went to the bandage over the gunshot wound on his side. He had almost forgotten about it.

He looked up and identified Hercules, the Northern Cross, the archer Sagittarius. What was it Grace said that night back on the Dry Cimarron Highway?

Somehow things don't seem as important out here.

Maybe she was right.

He felt like he could sleep. A foreign, unsettling feeling. Cricket song surrounded him, repetitious and lulling. He stretched out on his back, shifted away from a pebble that dug into his spine, then folded his hands behind his head and stared up at the sky in time to see a falling star.

Catch a falling star and –

Ray honey.

"Gin," he whispered, and closed his eyes.

21: Forgiveness

Geothermal mineral water eased Grace's weary body as the sun set and stars ignited the night sky. The smell of sage pooled in the air, though the smudge had gone out. The soothing burble of the falls massaged raw nerves. She drew in measured breaths, pulling therapeutic steam deep into her lungs. Calm infused her soul.

Her thoughts drifted. Echoes from the past ebbed and flowed.

Remember where you come from, baby girl.

"I do, Papa." Her voice sounded distant and youthful.

She ran through a waist-high field of alfalfa, the stems tugging at her cotton dress and tickling her palms as she held her arms outstretched. The sun warmed her head;

seedpods stuck to her brown skin.

Grandma James hunched at the battered upright piano, her gnarled fingers striking ivory while her sweet, high voice warbled "Soon I Will Be Done." The rhythmic creak of Grandpa James keeping time in the Mission rocker quieted a child's tumultuous heart.

The languid flow of Papa's words like honey as he coaxed her and brother to sleep with sonnets and tales of love and tragedy and justice.

Green felt and the crisp flutter of cards, like startled pigeon wings.

~~~

Ray opened his eyes to more stars than he'd ever seen. It didn't feel like he'd been asleep all that long, but the sky had turned midnight black. Disorientation prickled his skin. The stars didn't look right. *I'm in the desert*, he reminded himself, and sat up.

The blue sphere of Earth rose on a cratered, barren horizon, an image he had seen dozens of times after Apollo 8's historic lunar orbit. Fear and astonishment jolted through him. "I'm on the goddamn moon."

He grabbed a fistful of fine, gray dust and let it filter through his fingers, stirring up a mini storm. He'd read that dust took its time settling on the moon because of low gravity. He was still naked. No special equipment. No spacesuit. *What's keeping me from floating away? Shouldn't I be cold? How am I able to breathe?*

"Hi, Dad."

He choked on a startled gasp and turned to see Benny a couple yards away – Terminator t-shirt and leather pants, bare feet, the quilt from Rose's cabin over his arm. "How'd you get up here?" Ray asked. A ridiculous question that he followed with another. "How did *we* get here?"

Benny shrugged. "A dream."

Ray cupped his hands over his privates and quickly glanced around. "Is Grace here too?"

Benny giggled. "No, Dad." His bare feet kicked up dust clouds as he moved closer and wrapped the quilt around Ray's shoulders. It smelled of sage. "Rose let me use this."

"She's a spooky lady."

Benny gave a beauteous smile. "She's magic."

Ray couldn't argue with that. No other way to explain the two of them on the moon, having this conversation. "Why are we here?" he asked.

"It's safe."

Not sure how to digest that response, Ray realized his boy took being on the moon too calm for a first-timer. It occurred to him he might be seeing the moon from inside Benny's head, and wondered just how much, or little, Rose actually had to do with any of this. "Have you been here before, son?"

"Yeah." Benny sat cross-legged beside him, sending more dust into the atmosphere. "Sometimes other places."

"What other places?"

"I don't know the names."

"Other planets?"

"Da-a-ad."

"Sorry." Too many questions. Ray suspected a lot of those other places had hard-to-pronounce fictional names from episodes of Star Trek and Star Wars movies. He took in the magnificence of planet Earth, a blue oasis. "Sure is somethin'," he breathed.

"Home."

Ray's insides tightened. He looked at his son. "Do you miss our place in Ohio?"

Benny's shoulders rose and fell in a long, deep sigh. "I miss Mama."

Mama, not the house. Ray nodded. "So do I."

"She talks to you."

"Yeah, about that..." He didn't know how much he wanted to tell his boy.

"Mama doesn't talk to me because she's mad

at me."

Surprised, Ray asked, "Why would she be mad at you?"

Tears pooled in Benny's eyes. "I killed her."

Ray stilled, his son's utter sorrow and conviction so unexpected it locked his brain off from his vocal cords. *How could he possibly think he killed his mama? I'm the one to blame for her death. I'm the one who didn't wake up while she slipped away.* Would he ever get the image of her lifeless face out of his head? The cloudiness of her once vibrant green eyes? He choked back the guilt lodged in his throat and said softly, "Your mama died in her sleep."

Benny's face reddened and tears spilled down his cheeks. "I know! I broke her vase and made her sad and her color got dark like a storm and I didn't tell anybody because I didn't want them to call me stupid," he drew in a jerky breath, "and then she died."

Too much information poured from the boy to take in at once. Ray chose one thing to focus on. "What do you mean, her color got dark?"

"I see people's colors. Here," Benny circled his head with a stubby, impatient finger, "like angel halos, only bigger."

"Auras." Ray couldn't say how he knew of the phenomenon – probably something Gin

254

told him about or read to him when he was only half listening. "And your mama's got dark after you broke her vase?"

"Yes!"

One word, spoken clear, without any of his usual thick-tongued pronunciation. Ray realized Benny's speech lacked the characteristics of Down syndrome, as though being on the moon or, more accurately, in a dream state, freed him of his disability. That answered a question long on Ray's mind about how Benny heard himself when he had private conversations in his head.

And seeing his mama's dark aura explained why the boy had looked at Gin so strange in her last days. Had the aura been a portent of her brain aneurysm? Would knowing about it have changed anything?

Hell no. Benny was right. Nobody would have believed him. Besides, Ray didn't think there was any connection. To prove it to himself, he asked, "What color is my aura?"

"I don't see them all the time. I don't know why." Benny's voice became small.

"But you saw mine the day you said we should go to the Grand Canyon, didn't you?"

Benny wiped at his tears and nodded.

"And it was dark because I was sad," Ray

guessed, though it wasn't much of a guess. He could see the answer on his son's face.

"I didn't want you to die."

Ray felt pressure at the backs of his eyes as the tragic significance of Benny's nightmares hit him. A grieving boy who blamed himself for his mama's death. A boy scared of losing his daddy too. A boy making up for a past mistake the only way he knew how. Ray had been so busy wallowing in his own grief and guilt, he'd been blind to the depth of his son's trauma.

Get your head out of your ass, he told himself, *and take care of your boy the way he's been trying to take care of you*.

"Lot's of people get sad," Ray explained. "That doesn't mean they're going to die."

"Mama did."

"Because a blood vessel burst in her brain, like when you blow up a balloon too far and it pops. It happened so fast, nobody could have done anything about it." He realized what he just said, and paused.

There was nothing you could do, Ray honey.

He softly answered, "Because it happened too fast."

Benny gave him a stunned look. Then Ray saw understanding in his son's eyes. He felt a hand cup his cheek, as warm and gentle as his wife's touch, but it was Benny consoling him.

"I'm sorry we couldn't save her, Daddy."

We.

Ray drew in a ragged breath and his tears broke loose. "Me too, son." He pulled Benny to him and wrapped the blanket around them both. "Me too."

~~~

Grace returned to the hogan before dawn, her body loose, her troubled mind at peace. She would allow Doctor Medford credit for his prescription to relax, but her peace of mind went beyond soaking in a tub of hot mineral water. She praised God for leading her on this journey of discovery, for showing her the way back to the woman she thought she'd never see again.

While Benny slept, she and Rose set their chairs out under the stars and talked. Grace told how she came to be hooked up with a *bilagáana* – white man – and his son. Rose chuckled at Grace's car thieving and told about the time she drove her brother Michael's pickup into the ditch to avoid running over a snake. "It was his own fault. He told me people who killed snakes got crooked teeth."

"It must have worked," Grace said. "You

have beautiful teeth."

Rose laughed.

When the moon hung low and the first streaks of dawn colored the sky, they took their chairs back inside and Rose brewed coffee on a propane camp stove.

"Your friend should return soon," she said and poured Grace a tall mug.

"Thank you." Grace inhaled the dark roast aroma. With the first sip, she could hear Ray say, *Man, that's good*. He'd be right, too.

~~~

The pale blue of early dawn filtered through Ray's eyelids. Birdsong assured him he was back on Earth. Back in the desert. Every muscle in his body, every pore, even his hair and eyeballs, felt rested. For the first time in two months, he slept.

And he dreamed. God, what a dream. Dried tears crusted the corners of his eyes. Lightness filled his chest. He sat up and glanced around. "Ben?" But of course his son wasn't there. That was the way of dreams.

He saw the moon fading on the horizon and smiled.

~~~

Grace took her mug of coffee outside to look for any sign of Ray. The clear, pastel canopy promised another warm day as two sparrows sang back and forth to each other.

Movement in the distance caught her attention. She leaned forward and squinted, then jerked upright. "Mercy." Ray had his back to her, flashing his pale behind as he bent to pull on his briefs.

A pitiful, thin behind. *That man needs some meat on his bones.* Too much coffee, not enough home cooking, be her guess. The only thing comes of fast-food breakfast sandwiches is gas. Grace chuckled into her mug at the memory.

When all this was over, she'd like to take the boys home with her, cook them up a big pot of beans and greens thick with pickled pork rib tips. Bake her famous coconut cake that never failed to earn praise at church potlucks. She made the best fried chicken in Little Rock, too, but she suspected there be more to Benny's menu preference than just his taste buds. She wouldn't disrespect the child's memory of his mama by trying to compete. She knew how fragile memories could be.

Grace turned and went inside before Ray could catch her watching him.

~~~

Benny woke on Rose's bed. He petted the

soft blanket she had put over him, the blanket he took to his dad on the moon. He never shared a dream with anybody before. He didn't know how it happened, it just did.

He could hear his mama now, heard her tell Dad nothing could be done about her dying. It surprised Benny that his dad blamed himself. Then Mama whispered, "You're the smartest, bravest boy I know, Benjamin Ray Colton. Take care of your daddy. Be happy."

Hearing her pretty voice warmed his insides. Knowing she wasn't mad at him made the hurt of missing her not so bad. He pushed back the blanket and got up. Grace and Rose looked at him from the table.

Grace said, "Good morning, sugar."

Benny rubbed his eyes and smiled. "Hi, honey." Then Daddy walked in, tall and strong and glowing. Benny felt his heart grow big. "Yellow," he said.

His dad stopped and looked at him like he didn't understand.

"Your color halo," Benny explained. "It's yellow."

Dad grinned and held his arms out. Benny went to him.

22: Desert Dustup

Ray followed his son to the table and snuck a quick glance at the boy's pant cuffs for moon dust. It was probably a good thing he didn't see any, but still, he couldn't help feeling a little disappointed.

Grace sat at the table, nursing a mug of coffee.

"Good morning," he said, sliding a chair out.

Her gaze bounced off his as she answered "good morning" back.

Ray couldn't recall ever seeing a black person blush before, so when Grace's skin flushed pinker than usual, he paused and studied the smile she hid behind the rim of her coffee mug. Then it hit him, she must have seen him dressing. He'd been surprised at how close he was to Rose's place when the sun came up, close enough for Grace to see his scrawny, naked ass. His face grew hot. He quickly looked away and sat.

Rose brought him a mug of coffee. "Enjoy your walk?" she asked.

The woman still made him uncomfortable, even though he was pretty sure she didn't have anything to do with the moon dream. *Did she see my scrawny, naked ass too?* He avoided meeting her eyes and said, "It was tolerable."

She had a pleasing laugh, as deep and rich as her coffee. Benny giggled and Ray felt his own mouth pull into a smile.

A low rumble outside interrupted the moment. It grew louder as it approached.

"The Black Pearl!" Benny shouted, and ran to open the door.

"That will be my little brother," Rose said and followed Benny outside. Ray and Grace brought up the rear.

A lean, brown-skinned man in faded jeans and a blue-plaid shirt, his long braid flying behind him, drove the Harley to within a few feet of the door and stopped. As the trailing dust settled, he swung off the bike and flashed Rose a broad grin. "I got your call."

"You called him?" Ray asked. "When? How?" He thought of the eagle and stopped short of looking up at the sky.

"Last night," Rose said. "On my cell phone." She drew the device from the pocket of her skirt and waved it at him. "You should think about getting one."

Benny marched forward and thrust out his hand. "Benjaminraycolton."

Ray expected Rose's brother to shy away from the boy's straightforwardness – most people did – but the man took Benny's hand in a firm shake and said, "Please to meet you. My name's Henry." He released Benny's hand and gave Rose a hug.

"This is Ray," she said. "He asks a lot of questions."

Henry shook Ray's hand. "Nice shirt."

"And this is their traveling companion Grace," Rose said.

Henry smiled and nodded. He looked at Ray and said, "I fixed your flat."

"I see that." His helmet was strapped to the backrest, too. "Thanks. How'd you get the bike over here?"

"The road." Henry jabbed a thumb over his shoulder and Ray saw the dirt lane leading up to the cabin. Somehow he'd missed it before. "You didn't think the *hooghan* just dropped outta the sky, did you?"

Stranger things have happened, Ray thought, catching the smirk brother and sister exchanged at his expense. "What do I owe you for the tire?"

"Nothin', man. It was worth it to get to ride again. And with the sidecar," he shook his head, "what a trip. You know anything about the crazy white man about a mile out, throwing underwear across the desert?"

Ray's stomach tightened. "That would be mine."

"The dude looked pretty pissed off," Henry said.

"Yeah, I'll bet he was. He still there?"

"Last I saw." Henry looked at his sister. "You're right. He does ask a lot of questions."

Benny snickered.

"Come inside," Rose said. "I'll put on another pot of coffee."

~~~

Grace could tell by the look on Ray's face he'd made up his mind about something. She thought she knew what that something was, so she stayed behind as Benny followed Rose and Henry inside.

"I'm going to return the money," Ray told her once they were alone. "I'd like you to keep Benny out of the way in case there's anymore shooting."

"Johnny's not going to be happy about some of that money bein' spent," Grace said. "What makes you think his aim won't be any better the next time?"

"I'll have to risk it. Maybe he'll agree to take the Harley as partial payment."

"No!" Benny's shout from the open doorway set the hairs on Grace's neck to standing up. "The Black Pearl's ours!" he bawled, and made a rush for the motorcycle.

Ray blocked the charge, wrapped his arms around Benny's shoulders and attempted to calm him, but the boy put up a struggle.

"Black Pearl ours! My money! Finders keepers!"

He said more but heated emotion rendered his words unintelligible to Grace's ears. He whipped himself into a tantrum that Ray seemed to have no idea how to manage. Grace didn't abide tantrums, no matter the child's age or special needs. Her own children learned quick not to go there.

"Hush that!" she snapped.

Benny stopped his ranting and gave her a startled look. Then he began to cry.

Grace resisted the impulse to gather him up and comfort him. "I said hush," she repeated, her voice lower but no less un-giving.

Benny gulped, swiped at his face with the backs of his hands, and fell quiet.

"That's better," Grace said. "Now then," she looked from Benny to Ray, "I may have another way out of this predicament."

Ray stared at her, waiting. Whatever happened last night in the desert changed him, like the weight he'd been packing around eased. But grief left its mark on those blue eyes of his as they all but pleaded with her for help.

Grace prayed she didn't let him down.

~~~

Ray forced himself to hold his tongue while Grace suggested gambling the rest of the money to win back what they spent. He flashed to the night she told him she sometimes forgets things that happened years ago. And there was the phone number she couldn't remember. Her own phone number. When she stopped talking and looked to him for a response, all he could say was, "You haven't played poker in a long time."

"Like riding a bicycle."

Either she had a hell of a poker face, or she really believed what she said. If Ray hadn't spent the night on the moon with his son, conversing with his dead wife, he would have called her crazy. Trading the Harley made a lot more sense. If she lost the rest of the money in a poker game, the Harley wouldn't be enough. Then what?

"What makes you sure this'll work, Grace?"

"Ain't no guarantees," she said. "But I think I know who can swing the odds in my favor."

"Who?"

"Johnny."

Crap.

"I have a hunch he got his gambling debt at a poker table."

"Do it, Dad."

Ray looked at Benny, surprised to see him still standing there. Did the boy sense something? *Or am I grasping at straws?* He looked back at Grace. The woman was in this mess because of him. Because she trusted him. He could at least return the courtesy. He trusted her with his son; something told him he could trust her with this, too.

And he'd bet money she wasn't losing her mind.

"Alright then."

~~~

Ray parked the Harley next to a yucca waving a pair of white briefs like a flag of truce. Several yards away, on the shoulder of the two-lane headed south, sat the silver car coated in red dust. He didn't see Johnny anywhere.

Ray shut the Harley off and dismounted. He retrieved his underwear from the yucca and spotted one of his t-shirts caught at the base of a rock. When he picked it up, he saw the shirt had been ripped in two. The other half lay a short distance away. The hairs on his neck prickled. *Pretty pissed off* might be putting Johnny's mood mildly. Ray decided his laundry could wait. Better to confront the guy head on than risk a shot in the back. Still clutching his briefs and torn shirt, he made his way toward the car.

Johnny stepped from behind a large rock a few feet in front of him. The man's tight-fitting mustard yellow shirt and shiny black pants looked so out of place in the serene Red Rock setting, Ray missed a step. Then he saw the gun Johnny held against the right leg of those shiny pants. Ray knew he should call a truce, maybe wave his briefs in surrender. But when he looked up from the gun to the smug expression on the asshole's face, he forgot about what he *should* do. He remembered Grace bound and bruised. He remembered the potshots that could have killed any one of them. The wound on his side pulsed and anger roiled inside him. The asshole didn't have a right to that smug look. Ray dropped his laundry and rushed him.

Johnny's mouth popped open like he had something to say, but Ray didn't give him the chance. Growling, he wrapped his arms tight around that ugly yellow shirt and propelled the man backwards. Their feet tangled and Johnny *whumphed* flat on his back with Ray's full weight on top of him. The gun hit the dirt a few feet away.

Ray figured this must be what it felt like to ride a rodeo bull as Johnny bucked and twisted beneath him. He fought to catch his breath, the smell of onions and cheap cologne gagging. He fought to keep his neck from breaking. He fought with what seemed like half a dozen arms at once.

Then Johnny headed-butted him. Hard. Ray's head snapped back and pain radiated behind his eyeballs. Johnny shoved out from under him and staggered to his feet. He lunged for the gun, but Ray grabbed his ankle and the man fell face first into a boulder.

Johnny's head bounced, then his entire body turned in slow motion. He fell back against the boulder and slid to his butt in the dirt. Blood oozed from his nostrils and the rock rash on his forehead. "Son of a bitch," he wailed, delicately feeling at his nose. "I think you busted it this time."

Ray figured that made them even. He struggled to his hands and knees. "You didn't think I'd give you a chance to shoot me again, did you?"

"I shot you?"

"Got the gouge in my side to prove it."

Johnny went back to prissing with his nose. "I was just tryin' to scare you. I don't even like guns."

"Then you won't mind if I get rid of this." Ray crawled over to the pistol – a Taurus .40 cal – and popped the magazine. He hesitated, considered his current lack of a firearm, then flashed on Benny and tossed the gun into the brush. He emptied the magazine, letting the cartridges fall where they may, and tossed the magazine in the opposite direction. One of his torn t-shirts lay within reach. He wadded it into a ball and chucked it at Johnny. "Here. I've found cotton to be quite absorbent."

As luck would have it, the shirt flew straight at Johnny's face. He jerked and struck the back of his head on the boulder. "Ow, man!"

Ray sniggered. "Good thing you got a hard

head." He hoisted himself onto a low, flat rock. Sitting with his hands on his knees, he regarded Johnny. "I see ya got a new set of wheels."

"It's a rental. You know what it's gonna cost to fix my 'Stang?"

"I've got car issues of my own to worry about. What now?"

Johnny held the t-shirt to his nose, his voice muffled as he answered, "Now you give me my money instead of your laundry."

"Here's the problem," Ray said. "I had to use some of the money – "

"*My* money."

" – to buy that bike over there." Ray nodded toward the Harley. "My car crapped out and we need to be in Vegas by tonight."

"So do I." Johnny lowered the t-shirt, the blood from his nose staunched for the time being. "If I don't get that money, *all* of it, to Vegas by midnight, I'm a dead man. You understand? A *dead* man."

"So it was a pay-off."

Johnny gave a harsh laugh. "Do I look like a guy who walks around with that kind of dough for no good reason?"

The asshole had a point. "Why the garbage can?"

Johnny eyed him as though trying to decide how much to tell him. "I thought I was being followed."

"By who? We were in the middle of nowhere, for crap sake."

"Yeah, well, that's what I thought too, 'til Mr. Tony's muscle caught up with me."

"Mr. Tony?"

"The guy I owe the money to," Johnny said impatiently. "Shit, man, you ask a lot of questions."

"So I've been told."

"That pirate with the gun isn't hiding behind one of these rocks, is he?"

"He's safe."

"Kid's got guts, I'll give 'im credit. Some day you'll have to explain to me why he tried to rob that store. But right now I've got more important things to think about. I owe a lot of money I apparently no longer have to a man with a serious lack of humor."

"How'd you come to owe Mr. Tony so much?"

"Poker."

Ray smiled. *Sombitch, Grace nailed it.*

"It's not funny, man!"

"It's perfect. Where in Vegas do we find this guy?"

"We?" Johnny slanted him a wary look, his face scrunched against the sun. It started his nose bleeding again. "Ain't no *we* about it. *I* deliver the money and hope to hell Mr. Tony will accept a Harley and sidecar as part of the payment."

"What if I told you there's another way?"

Johnny mopped at the blood on his upper lip. "Only other way is if you can shit money like the goose that laid the golden egg."

"There ya go pissing me off again," Ray warned. "I'm trying to have a civil conversation with you, find a way we can all come out of this smelling good, and you're actin' like an asshole."

"Asshole's my middle name."

Without a word, Ray got to his feet and made for the Harley.

"Hey! Come back here!"

Ray shouted over his shoulder, "I don't waste my time talkin' to assholes," and continued to walk away.

Johnny plowed into him from behind and propelled them both to the ground, face first. Ray ate dirt before he got twisted around and flipped Johnny's weight off him. He tried to pop to his feet but scrambled sideways like a crab, until his legs gave out and he did a slow-motion sit. A few feet away, Johnny sat up and swatted at the dust coating his black pants.

Ray spat and asked, "Feel better?"

"They're ruined."

"Cooperate and you'll have enough to buy a new pair when it's over, maybe even get your Mustang fixed."

Johnny stopped and looked at him, shook his head. "Man, where'd you get that ugly shirt?"

Ray didn't answer.

Johnny got the message. "So what's this plan of yours?"

23: The Stardust

US-93 between Kingman and Boulder City had to be the longest, hottest, straightest stretch of boredom Grace ever experienced. She baked inside her leathers, self-basted in sweat. Every now and again, Benny's head bobbed, bounced off Ray's back and jerked up. Ray appeared not to notice, locked in a stupor as he held the motorcycle's speed well above the limit. If not for the hot air pushing at her, Grace would have swore they weren't moving.

The monotony gave her time to go over what she knew about Mr. Tony, the man she hoped to strike up a game with. According to Johnny, people called him the Roman and he owned a small establishment in east Las Vegas, off the Strip. "Small establishment" could mean any number of things, but that didn't much concern Grace. She and Papa played most of their games in back rooms and basements.

Mr. Tony's poker moniker interested her more.

"Why do people call him the Roman?" she asked Johnny as he sipped the coffee Rose shoved at him before joining the others outside the hogan. Grace had to hand it to Ray, the man looked plenty the worse for wear. Her observation stopped shy of sympathy.

"Dude likes to quote Shakespeare, mostly *Julius Caesar*, from what I hear. Guess he thinks it makes him sound *intellectual*. Half the time nobody knows what he's talking about."

Grace felt that shiver and slide up her arms. "You're not familiar with the Bard?"

"Who?"

"Not important," she said, though Papa's fondness for *Shakespeare's Complete Works* over the Holy Bible, much to Mother's annoyance, might be *very* important. "What's this Roman's game?" she asked.

"No limit Texas Hold'em."

"Hold Me Darling."

"Excuse me?"

Grace smirked at the sudden high color on Johnny's cheeks. "That's what they used to call the game 'fore Texas caught on."

Johnny's gaze narrowed. "Have you ever played Texas Hold'em?"

In her day, seven-card stud was the preferred game – counting cards, watching betting patterns. Hold'em was more about reading people, intestinal fortitude and bluffing. "It's all poker," she said with a shrug.

Johnny didn't appear too comfortable with her answer. "I'm a dead man."

Grace chose to ignore his skeptical nature. "Does Mr. Tony play tight or loose?"

"The Roman plays so tight, he can't fart." Johnny cleared his throat. "If you know what I mean."

"Yes, I get the picture." Tight games took longer, meant the man be a careful player. "Does he cheat?"

"Not against me," Johnny answered, his tone defensive.

Mr. Tony, a.k.a. the Roman, ran an honest game, or Johnny wasn't sharp enough to spot a cheat at work. "He got a tell?"

Johnny shook his head, took another sip of coffee. "I played until I was too deep to climb out, watching for it, but the man plays cool enough to freeze your ba—"

"*Lord* have mercy, I get the picture."

"Sorry."

"Where'd you get the money to pay him back?"

"I rounded my way to Oklahoma until I had enough. Took me a while, which is why Mr. Tony's getting antsy."

"How much of that hundred thousand is interest?"

"Half."

Grace sucked her teeth. She sat across the table from her share of people like Johnny who didn't know when to cut their losses and walk away. Some played to win; others played because they were addicted and let emotions rule good sense. She'd seen babies go hungry because their folks stopped at a poker game that went on 'til the grocery money ran out.

"You married, Johnny?"

He ducked his head. "Naw. Guess I've been as unlucky in the romance department as I have been at winning poker."

"Luck ain't got nothin' to do with it, young man. You got any cards on you?"

He pulled a battered deck from his shirt pocket.

"Walk me through a couple hands."

Johnny looked like he couldn't make up his mind whether to cry or curse. Finally he muttered "I'm a dead man" again, and began shuffling the cards.

After Johnny refreshed her memory on the rules of Hold'em, he refilled his coffee cup and took it outside, leaving Grace alone with the card deck and her thoughts.

The cards felt comfortable in her hands. It surprised her how much so. The notion that she'd like to play again came on while she soaked in Rose's hot springs tub. With her mind drifting from one memory to the next, she found herself wondering if she still had what it took. She'd like to honor Papa's legacy by proving she did. The possibility Johnny's debt came from a poker table had been nothing more than a hunch, but the odds had been in her favor. She prayed they stayed that way. She prayed for an opportunity to set things right. She prayed for guidance and clear thinking. And she prayed she remembered everything Johnny told her.

A change in the motorcycle's rhythm brought Grace out of her musings. Ray had slowed for the winding descent to Hoover Dam.

~~~

Benny never saw anything like Hoover Dam before. The road went right over the top, and people walked around taking pictures. Dad said there wasn't time to stop, but traffic went really slow, so Grace got his camera out of the saddlebag and he took pictures from the back of the Black Pearl. Daddy pointed to the bypass bridge being built and Benny took pictures of that too.

Johnny followed behind in the silver car. He wanted Benny to ride with him, "for insurance," he said, but Dad said no way in hell, take it or leave it. Johnny sounded funny when he talked, like he had a cold, because of the cotton plugging his nose. Rose fixed him up before they left. Benny could tell she didn't like Johnny – not the way she liked Dad. She wasn't very careful when she shoved the cotton into Johnny's nose holes. Even though it made Benny laugh, he felt kind of sorry for Johnny. He remembered what it felt like to breathe swimming pool water and thought that's how Johnny looked, like he couldn't breathe without something bad happening.

Benny touched the front of his jacket and felt the necklace Rose gave him inside. She called it a dreamcatcher and explained how bad dreams got tangled up in the web and only good dreams got through. "You won't have any more nightmares," she said. He didn't tell her he already knew that because his mama told him so. The necklace was pretty, like Rose, and he would wear it always to remind him of her. Grace got a bundle of leaves and sticks. "For emergencies," Rose said. It didn't make any sense to Benny, but Grace must have understood because she gave Rose a hug and called her Sister. Rose gave Dad a small jar of ointment in case he got shot again. Dad's face turned red. Benny thought if his dad didn't miss Mama so much, he and Rose might have a romance. She was a babe.

~~~

When Grace got her first good look at Las Vegas, the enormity of it staggered her breath. A dusty haze of construction shrouded the city in the afternoon's hot flush.

Lord Jesus, what have I gotten myself into?

~~~

"Stop!" Grace shrieked.

Ray hit the brakes, Benny slid into him, tires squalled behind them and the bumper of Johnny's car kissed the bike's rear fender. Bike and sidecar jumped the curb, sending a handful of pedestrians scrambling out of the way. Ray killed the engine and looked to Grace for an explanation. She stared at the gutted shell of a high-rise fenced off from the public.

The Stardust, according to the sign.

For all the fuss, it didn't look like much, Ray thought. By the slump to Grace's shoulders, he figured she thought the same thing.

"Can't be," she said, shaking her head. "It's in the right place, but it don't look nothin' like the Stardust."

"Oh, that's the Stardust," Johnny said. He'd gotten out of his car and stood at the back of the bike. "It's wired to come down early tomorrow morning. Then it'll just be another pile of dinosaur rubble to haul off."

Ray shot him a frown. "Shut up, asshole."

"Yeah, shut up," Benny echoed.

Johnny gave them a puzzled look. "What? I'm just saying – "

"Hey!" somebody shouted from a passing vehicle. "You jerks can't park there!"

Ray saw Johnny's hand come up, ready to flip the driver off. "Don't," he warned.

Johnny looked from Ray, to Benny, to Grace, and dropped his hand. "Whatever. You guys ready to meet Mr. Tony?"

Ray looked to Grace. She had her sunglasses off and wiped at her eyes. When she met his gaze, he could see she'd composed herself. "We need to find this child something to eat and I need a place to freshen up. Then I have an outfit to buy."

~~~

Ray perched on the edge of a broke-down couch next to his son and idly picked at the remains of a forgettable dinner between his teeth. The vintage shop's air freshener didn't quite disguise the musty basement smell of old clothes. He didn't know what buying a secondhand outfit had to do with poker, but he made up his mind to trust Grace's judgment and, by God, that's what he was going to do.

Johnny didn't hang around, said he had business to take care of. "Meet me here," he handed Ray a card for a place called Roman's Bar & Burgers, "at seven-thirty. Don't even think about not showing."

The threat didn't hold much weight, coming from a skinny, dusty weasel with a broken nose. Grace had his money tucked in her purse, "For safe keeping," she told him. None of that mattered. Ray had no intention of backing out now. It didn't set right owing Johnny money, asshole or not. He was done running.

Benny belched softly. "'xcuse me."

"You're excused," Ray said.

"It stinks in here, Dad."

"Must be your breath blowin' back in your face."

Benny snickered. "*Your* breath."

"Naw. Never happened."

Their back-and-forth stopped short when Grace strolled out of the dressing room wearing a pajama-style pantsuit of large purple, orange and dark blue paisleys on a pink background, the long-sleeved jacket and wide, straight-legged pants bordered in a smaller, no-less colorful print the likes of which Ray hadn't seen in over four decades. It put the god-awful Aunt Georgie shirt he had to retire – after his tussle with Johnny – to shame.

She's gone off the deep end.

Grace pirouetted in her stocking feet and asked, "What do you think?"

Benny grinned. "Nice, honey."

Ray struggled to find a reaction that wouldn't get him slapped. He settled for, "It's bright."

"That it is."

"You planning to blind the man, then steal his money?"

Grace laughed and took another spin. "I plan to dazzle him with inexperience."

"By making him believe you're a tourist stuck in the sixties."

"Who thinks she knows more about poker than she does."

"Will he fall for that?"

"I hope not."

Ray rubbed at his forehead. The woman made him dizzy with her psychedelic twirling and double speak. "You lost me."

"Good. The plan is to keep Mr. Tony guessing too."

"While you take his money."

"You're catching on." She winked and turned toward the footwear section. "I need some ugly shoes to go with this ugly outfit."

~~~

If the Stardust didn't take Grace back in time, the '60s pantsuit did. She had decided to get as close as possible to the feel of that day, put herself in the moment, the *mood* for card playing. Weren't nothing she could do about not being twenty-three and svelte anymore, but the fluorescent paisley pantsuit helped. She forgot how comfortable the sweep of acrylic cloth could be. A pair of red espadrille slides topped with huge crimson flowers finished the affair. She drew the line at attempting to replicate the Jackie Kennedy bouffant, deeming it a once-in-a-lifetime experience.

She felt like showing off. "Seems a shame not to cruise the Strip and see the lights while we're here."

Ray checked Benny's watch. "We don't have

to meet Johnny for a while yet."

"Cool," Benny said.

Heat continued to hug the early evening air. They stowed their leather jackets and loaded onto the Harley. Grace wrapped a scarf around her tight up-do to keep it in place under her helmet. Ray looked right handsome in his stone-washed blue button-down, sleeves rolled, shirt tails fluttering loose in the breeze. Benny wore his Terminator t-shirt; Arnold Schwarzenegger straddling a black Harley ballooned behind a boy straddling a black Harley.

People called Vegas an oasis in the desert, but what Grace remembered as a pond of lights had grown to an ocean dominated by high-rises. The Stratosphere tower looked like something straight from the Seattle World's Fair. The Sahara, still standing, had changed considerably. Same for the infamous Riviera. Circus Circus, Slots A Fun, Sports World, all new. Anticipation charged the air as people milled from one opportunity to the next, seeking riches, entertainment, and cheap buffets. Vegas may have grown up, but some things never changed.

They drove by what remained of the Stardust again and Grace's heart ached. The ugly towering shell set for demolition could be any old building in the way of progress. The round, star-studded sign that welcomed her and Papa years ago no doubt gathered dust in a neon bone yard, alongside the high-heeled Silver Slipper, illuminated by hundreds of light bulbs, that used to rotate atop the gambling hall next door.

What if there had been no Colton boys, no Johnny and bag of money, no Rose and claw foot tub? What if she had come all this way just for a broke down building?

Grace knew she wouldn't have survived the disappointment.

~~~

Benny couldn't believe his eyes. He blinked and looked again. Treasure Island! And a real pirate ship with babes on deck!

24: The Bard

By outward appearances, Roman's Bar & Burgers – an ebony building with reflective windows and neon beer signs – didn't look like a card-playing establishment. Could be the bar was a front to control who got into the back room, maybe slowed authorities long enough to hide evidence of crooked dealings in a basement. Grace had prepared herself for those possibilities. Still, she took comfort from Ray's hand at her elbow. Benny followed close enough to be his daddy's shadow, his pirate hat tipped low as a gunslinger's Stetson.

Johnny, dressed to the teeth in polished black, his dishwater blond hair slicked down, waited for them at the corner of the building. He quirked an eyebrow at Grace's outfit, but held his tongue as he led them down a narrow alley to a steel side door with half a dozen locks and a peephole. Grace felt Ray's hand tense.

"We're not going in the front?" he challenged.

"That's for nobodies," Johnny said.

"You mean nobodies who don't owe a wad of money to the boss."

Grace sensed it wouldn't take much provocation from either man to have them going at it again. Like two sticks of dynamite dancing around a lit match. Johnny pounded the door with the side of his fist and she flinched.

Ray leaned close and whispered, "You don't have to do this."

She pulled her shoulders back and drew in a deep breath. "Yes. I do."

~~~

Ray didn't like it one bit. Not one bit. He wished to God he hadn't buried the Smith & Wesson, wished he felt its weight and authority tucked into the waistband of his leather pants. Even Johnny's cheap .40 cal would do right now.

Locks snapped and the steel door swung open.

Benny pressed against him. "Dad?"

Ray reached back and put a hand to the boy's arm. "Stay behind me."

A giant of a black man in a cream-colored suit – had to be tailor-made to fit a body that size – filled the doorway. His dark eyes swept over them. If this was Mr. Tony, Ray could see why Johnny believed himself a dead man.

"Mr. Tony don't allow strangers in the back," the man said in a voice as large as his suit size. "You know that, Johnny."

"This is business, Moon. My friends and I have a business proposition for the Roman."

"Only business he's interested in is the money you owe him."

"I've got until midnight to pay up, right?"

The big man nodded – a slow, guarded movement.

Johnny thrust out his left arm, exposing a large gold watch, and made a show of studying it. "That gives us four hours and thirteen minutes to lay new business on the table. We're looking for a game."

Grace took a half-step forward in spite of Ray's restraining hold, and said, "A very *special* game." She brought her purse to her bosom and gave it a pat.

Good God, Ray thought, did she just bat her eyes at the man? Even more amazing, Moon's face went soft and dopy in response. He didn't seem the least bit interested in the purse full of money. Ray chewed the inside of his cheek to keep from smirking.

"A game worth a lot of money," Johnny added.

Moon ignored the weasel and smiled at Grace. "I'll see what I can do." He pulled back inside and closed the door.

Ray released an amused, "Damn."

Grace elbowed him and whispered, "Hush now. I'm workin' my wiles."

"I see that."

"If you're going to distract me, you can wait out here."

"No, ma'am. I ain't lettin' you out of my sight. I can keep a poker face."

"Good, because I'd really like to have you in the room with me, case things go south."

"Ben and I got your back."

The door opened and Moon invited them in. All but Benny. "You know the rules," Moon said, blocking the boy's entry with an arm the size of a steel girder . "No minors allowed."

Why Ray hadn't thought of that earlier baffled him. Maybe because somewhere along this crazy trip, he'd stopped thinking of his son as a child. A minor. "I'm not leaving him out here alone," he told the big man.

"And you're not bringing him inside," Moon replied.

"I'll hang with the kid," Johnny said.

Ray scowled. "You?"

Johnny shoved his hands into his pockets. "I'm in no hurry to face Mr. Tony. And she," he nodded toward Grace, "has what's left of my money anyway."

Ray shook his head. "No. After all that's happened, why should I trust you?"

"Come on, man. What am I going to do? Where 'm I gonna go?"

The guy had a point. Ray still didn't like it. Every bone in his body told him they needed to stick together, father and son. But there was Grace to think about too. She said it herself, she wanted him in the room in case things went bad. Torn, he glanced down at her. She opened her mouth to speak, no doubt to tell him she'd be okay, that he should stay with his son, but Benny's hand on his arm pulled Ray's attention away, and anything Grace had been about to say went unsaid.

"'kay, Dad."

Ray looked into his son's eyes and saw the maturity that had him forgetting the boy was only eleven. In that moment, he realized it didn't matter whether or not he trusted Johnny. He trusted his son. Still, he asked, "Are you sure?" and realized he had once again quoted Louise's last words before she tromped on the convertible's gas peddle and sent herself and Thelma into the great beyond. It left an unsettled feeling in his stomach.

"Yeah, Dad. Grace needs you."

The boy made sense. Ray turned to Johnny. "You let anything happen to him – "

"Don't worry, man. I'm still nursin' the last broke nose you gave me."

"I'll do more than break your nose, damn it."

"Da-a-ad."

Ray stood down. "Alright then."

Benny tugged him close, cupped a hand to his ear and whispered, "Watch cowboy."

"Cowboy?"

"Yeah."

"What cow—"

"It's not good to keep Mr. Tony waiting," Moon cut in.

Ray made to wave the man off, but Benny's tug on his arm drew his attention back. "'kay, Dad. Moon is safe."

Ray stared at his son, his brain hung up on the words the boy had said to him last night in their dream. "How..."

Benny grinned and pushed him toward the door, where the safe man named Moon waited. Ray found himself wishing Gin would talk to him right about now, help him make sense of these strange and confusing times, tell him what the hell to do. But all he heard was the steel door slam shut between him and his son.

~~~

Benny stared at the closed door, disappointed he didn't get to watch Grace play poker. He knew she would be okay, though, as long as Dad stayed with her. And Moon liked her – Benny saw it in the big man's face, like a giant teddy bear waiting for a hug. He wouldn't let anybody hurt Grace either.

"Hey, Captain Hook, you aren't packin', are ya?"

Benny turned around and gave Johnny his meanest look. Mama called it his stink-eye because it made his face squinty. "I'm Captain Jack Sparrow, stupid." But he said it too fast and Johnny stared at him like he didn't understand. Benny gave a disgusted sigh and mumbled, "No gun."

"Great. Where do you wanna go?"

"Treasure Island."

"What? No! Your dad would kill me. Let's go to Circus Circus."

~~~

Grace paused inside the card room door to steady herself. The smell of beer and neat whiskey from a mini-bar at the far wall, the clatter of poker chips and snap of cards at the half-dozen green oval tables, illuminated by low-hanging pendant lights and Tiffany-style shades, hit her senses with a wave of nostalgia. Poker was played here. A floor-to-ceiling cashier's cage stood in the corner. Framed stage posters on paneled walls, chocolate and cream houndstooth carpeting beneath their feet. The only thing missing was the pungent cloud of cigar smoke.

A hodgepodge of players – men and women wearing leisure suits to tank tops and shorts – occupied two thirds of the tables. Grace scanned their faces, half expecting to see her papa guarding his cards and sipping his ice water. He never drank while he played, said it dulled a man's mind. But the only black man in the room, outside of Moon, didn't look anything like Papa, though he did have a glass of what appeared to be ice water at his elbow. He caught her eyeing him, touched the brim of his smoke-gray cowboy hat to her, then went back to his game.

Ray gave her arm a light squeeze. "You

okay?"

His concern touched her heart. How many times had he asked about her well-being on this journey? He'd yanked her back from the precipice of panic she teetered on and looked after her like a brother. Better than a brother. A best friend. She patted his hand and replied, "I'm fine as frog's hair."

The muscles in his face relaxed around the crooked tilt of his mouth.

Mr. Tony sat alone at the back table. He might have been in his late thirties, early forties, his thick shock of dark brown hair spiked on top but trimmed neat around the sides. A day's growth gave his sharp-edged face a wan look against the red and black pinstripe shirt he wore. An audacious diamond ring flashed on one slender hand. He stood at their approach, as tall as Ray, and watched them from behind transparent amber glasses. Grace saw his eyes move from her to Ray, then back to her.

"Why are you interrupting my evening?"

"I'm here for a game," Grace said.

Mr. Tony regarded her. "Why should I take your money?"

"It's not my money. It's yours." Grace decided at a glance the dumb tourist ploy wouldn't work on this man. "I've got fifty grand that Johnny says belongs to you."

"His debt is twice that."

Grace sucked her teeth. "Indeed it is. I intend to double the fifty and pay back his debt, plus interest."

"Why does Johnny's debt matter to you?"

"This isn't about Johnny." *It's about me and my papa. It's about two boys from Ohio and all they done for me. It's about I don't approve of the way you like scarin' people.* "I'm just looking for a game," she told him.

"And if you lose?"

"I won't."

Mr. Tony sighed. "They all say that. Unfortunately, it's often untrue. You lose and I'm still out a hundred grand. I need more or there's no game."

Ray stepped forward. "I've got a Harley Softail with sidecar – "

"I dislike motorcycles."

"That's right, Johnny said you're into classic muscle cars."

Grace didn't remember Johnny saying anything of the sort. Had that been part of their conversation in the desert? Or was Ray doing a little gambling of his own? Either way, she could tell where he was headed and tried to stop him. "Ray, don't."

"I've got a '69 Olds 442," he said, ignoring her. "Burgundy mist, white accents, W-30 package, one owner...worth more than what that Harley'd go for."

"Where is it?"

"Albuquerque."

Mr. Tony waved a dismissive hand. "You're wasting my time, both of you."

Ray tensed and made as though to move closer. Grace cut him off, pressing in to rest her purse on the table. "Sugar, what have you got to lose? You don't play me, you're still out the money. You and I both know Johnny can't come up with another fifty grand by midnight. He's not that good."

"But you think you are." The man broke eye contact to glance at her purse.

Grace resisted a smile. "'Put money in thy purse,'" she challenged, quoting the villainous Iago from Shakespeare's *Othello*.

Mr. Tony's eyes lifted. "You've studied the Bard?"

"Enough to know poor Othello didn't have a chance. 'I am not what I am.'"

"'What conjuration...'"

"'And what mighty magic.'"

He stared at her for long seconds, then

without turning to look at Moon said, "Bring the lady her chips."

Ray leaned close and whispered, "What the hell was that all about?"

Grace patted his arm. "Don't you never mind. I got chips to purchase." She opened her purse and withdrew several bundles of bills, made sure her fingers brushed Moon's as she handed each one over to him, and said, "Thank you, dear."

The big man blushed.

Mr. Tony cleared his throat. "'Trust no agent, for beauty is a witch.'"

Much Ado About Nothing this time. "'Against whose charms faith melteth...'"

"'In blood.'"

She pasted a brazen smile on her face. "Let's hope it don't come to that."

Mr. Tony's tight laugh sent a chill across the table. Much as she enjoyed the Shakespeare banter, and was pleased with her recall, that tight laugh cautioned her to remember Johnny's fear of the man.

He motioned her to sit. "What's your name and what's your game?"

"My name is Grace." She sat and tucked her purse – now fifty grand lighter – in her lap. "I hear Texas Hold'em is popular."

Again with the long stare.

"We can play something else, if you prefer," she offered.

"Texas Hold'em is fine." He took his seat. "No limit, I presume?"

"You presume correct. I'd prefer this not take all night." She wiggled her hips a little, settling into her cushioned chair. "I have a date later."

25: Cowboys

Ray planted himself on the red vinyl couch against the wall, where he could keep an eye on Grace and Mr. Tony and the rest of the room at the same time. He had played some poker over the years, mostly in his Air Force days, but never with a stack of chips the likes of which Moon set in front of Grace. Those chips represented a lot of money. What if this didn't work?

He studied Grace at the table in her traffic-stopping pantsuit, her hair done up nice, spouting Shakespeare – *Shakespeare*, for God's sake – and shuffling the deck like she'd come home. He flashed on the evening in Albuquerque, when she told him he needed faith and he told her the only thing he had faith in was his son. That no longer held true,

301

he realized. His heart filled with more faith and love for Mrs. Grace Brown from Little Rock, Arkansas, than he thought possible.

No way this wouldn't work.

Benny said to watch cowboy. If a hat was all it took, the nickname applied to half a dozen men sitting around the room. One in particular caught Ray's attention – an old black man with skin like worn boot leather at the next table over. He wore a flashy blue, western-style shirt and stole glances at Grace from under the brim of a light gray cowboy hat. He may not be the only "cowboy" in the room, but he was the only one taking any interest in Grace.

Maybe she's worked her wiles on him too, Ray thought, and swiped at his mouth to stop the grin he felt coming on. He glanced at Moon standing off to Grace's side like an eager puppy waiting to please. It made Ray wonder what kind of woman Grace had been in her younger days, before she married a preacher and settled down. Traveling the country with her papa, in search of the next poker game, had there been romances in her male-dominated world? Broken hearts?

So much he didn't know about her, but their time together would be over soon. She'd head back to her family, and he'd take Benny on to the Grand Canyon.

Where he and his boy went from there, he didn't know. One thing he did know for certain, saying goodbye to Grace was going to be hard, especially for Benny, no matter how this night ended – good or bad.

~~~

Grace looked at her pocket cards – jack of clubs, ten of spades – and slid $800 into the pot. "Raise."

"Call." The diamond on Mr. Tony's finger flashed as he tossed in his chips.

Grace removed the top card from the deck and set it aside, then dealt the flop – king, ace, jack – pairing her jack.

Mr. Tony tapped the table. "Check."

"Eight hundred," Grace bet.

"Call," Mr. Tony said, bringing the pot to $3,200.

Grace burned the top card and dealt the turn – five of hearts.

Mr. Tony checked.

Grace checked and dealt the river – eight of spades.

"Twenty-four hundred," Mr. Tony said, and moved his chips in.

The sizable bet caused her to hesitate. She studied him, got nothing from his casual pose

– arms rested on the table, face expressionless – and weighed the odds he had paired the king or ace. "Fold."

"Wise decision." Mr. Tony flipped his pocket cards – king, ten – and collected the pot.

The deal went to the house, blinds posted – $200 and $400. Mr. Tony looked at his pocket cards and called.

Grace checked with a suited nine, four.

Mr. Tony dealt six, queen, jack on the flop.

Grace checked again.

"Bet five hundred," Mr. Tony said.

"Fold."

~~~

The Sand Pirate ship rocked back and forth like a giant swing under the Circus Circus Adventuredome, higher and higher. It didn't have babes, like the one at Treasure Island, but that was okay. Benny held onto his pirate hat with one hand and the bar across his lap with the other. He closed his eyes and imagined himself on a real ship, riding over giant ocean waves, the wind in his face. He smelled popcorn.

Johnny shouted, "Havin' fun, kid?"

"Yeah!"

~~~

Seven of diamonds on the turn.

"Check," Mr. Tony said.

Grace looked at her weak pocket cards. Indecision prickled her skin. "Fold." Another pile of chips went to her opponent's side of the table.

"'How like you this play?'" Mr. Tony asked as he dealt the next round.

Macbeth? No. *Hamlet*. It's from *Hamlet*. "'The lady protests too much,'" she replied, her tone snippy. *Protesting or not, I need to catch me some decent cards*. She looked at her hand – eight, deuce.

Mr. Tony raised $800.

"Fold."

Mr. Tony took the pot and Grace felt another layer of confidence slip away with her chips. She eyed her dwindling stack. *Dear Jesus in Heaven, what if I lose the rest of Johnny's money?*

~~~

Ray watched helpless as Grace folded another hand. Crap. This isn't going to work, he thought. He kept an eye on the door while his heart broke for his friend.

~~~

Grace's hands trembled as she shuffled the cards. Sweat prickled her skin and her chest felt tight. *I could use me some air*. She sensed Mr.

Tony staring at her, as though seeing through her facade. Her throat went dry. *I'm nothing but a silly old fool, hoping I can win against the likes of this man. A prideful, delusional old fool. What on earth was I thinking? I'm sorry, Papa. I –*

"Excuse me." The pretty young waitress from the bar set a glass of water with a wedge of lime next to Grace's elbow. "The gentleman over there asked that I give this to Cowboy's Girl."

Countless card rooms and countless games shivered through Grace. She hadn't been called Cowboy's Girl since her rounding days with Papa. But who...? She looked in the direction the waitress indicted. The ageless gentleman with skin like weathered rawhide tipped the brim of his cowboy hat back and gave her a good look at his periwinkle eyes.

Lord have mercy, the Black Saint. As I live and breathe.

He winked.

"Is there a problem?" Mr. Tony asked.

Grace realized she had paused mid-shuffle. She glanced at Ray and saw him half off the couch, a worried look on his face. She shot him a brief smile and nod to let him know she be alright.

The gentleman at the neighboring table

returned to his game.

"My apologies," she said to Mr. Tony. "I was overcome by a moment of déjà vu."

~~~

Benny went on the carousel and balloons with Johnny, even though he thought they were baby rides. Benny wanted to go on the rollercoaster, but Johnny said something about having a weak stomach. They went to the bumper cars instead. Johnny let him drive and laughed whenever they bumped another car.

"Run into that loser over there," Johnny said, so Benny did.

When their time was up on the bumper cars, they went to the midway and played a fishing game. Benny got frustrated when he couldn't make the hook go where he wanted it. "Fishing sucks," he mumbled.

"That's okay, kid," Johnny said. "Let's get some popcorn and take a load off."

"'kay."

They found a bench where they could sit and eat. "Can I ask you something, kid?"

"Yeah."

"Remember back in Santa Fe, when you shot at me?"

Benny frowned. "I didn't shoot at you."

"So you meant to put those holes in my

'Stang."

"Huh?" Benny hated when people used words he didn't know. Sometimes he thought they did it on purpose to make him feel like a dummy.

"My car...a Mustang...'Stang for short. You meant to put all those holes in the gas tank, didn't you?"

Benny looked away, felt his face get hot. "It didn't blow up."

Johnny laughed. It made Benny mad, but Johnny patted his shoulder like they were good buddies. "Sorry to tell ya this, kid, but that kind of thing only happens in the movies."

~~~

Papa used to say baffle your opponent. Do things he don't expect. Mr. Tony didn't expect her to win. Grace almost played into those expectations. Seeing a face from the past jolted her out of her tilt and got her back in the game. Once she stopped letting her emotions rule good sense, she won a few pots, managed to steal a couple more on bluffs. She raised pre-flop to make her cards appear strong whether they were or not. She limped in a time or two with a strong hand. The longer she played, the more natural it came to her.

Mr. Tony played it cool and tight as Gladys

Turner's upper lip in church. Never reached for his chips to call her bet before it be made. Didn't stare her down or play with his chips to distract or rush her. She looked for him to fiddle with that diamond headlight on his finger but it went untouched. The man didn't even double-check his pocket cards against the up cards as they were dealt. And except for spouting Shakespeare, he kept conversation to a minimum.

Moon refilled her water and lime, and brought a basket of pretzels from the bar, but Grace declined his offer to get her something from the grill.

"Raise," she said and tossed in $1,200.

"'All the perfumes of Arabia will not sweeten this little hand,'" Mr. Tony said, quoting *Macbeth* – Grace was sure of it this time – as he folded.

Grace collected the pot. "Mind telling me how you came to be called the Roman?"

"Pardon?"

"So far you've quoted from everything but *Julius Caesar*."

He smiled as though pleased by her observation. "*Julius Caesar* is not among my favorites, but one evening I found myself playing a man calling himself Caesar. I shouted

'Friends, Romans, countrymen, lend me your ears – '"

"'I come to bury Caesar, not to praise him.'"

"I've been stuck with the Roman ever since. I believe it's your deal."

End of small-talk.

~~~

Ray couldn't see any rhyme nor reason to the way Grace played, yet she had somehow bounced back from her shaky start and recovered a sizable amount of chips. He had to wonder how much was from skill and how much just plain luck.

The black man at the neighboring table collected his chips and stood. He reached the couch before his back had straightened. "Mind if I have a sit-down?"

Ray gave a nod and the man eased his bent frame onto the couch. Both knee joints popped. He leaned in close and whispered, "Her old man used to play it dat way.'"

Surprised, Ray asked, "You knew her papa?"

"Yep. Been a few years." The man flashed a smile too white to be his real teeth. "I was young and ambitious back then. Lost a couple paychecks to Cowboy Charlie."

Ray felt the room shift. "Cowboy?"

"Yep. Yep. Dat's what they called ol' Charlie.

Rode roughshod over youngsters like me. Didn't need no fancy hat, neither." He flicked the brim of his cowboy hat with a long, weathered finger.

Was Grace's papa the cowboy Benny said to watch? How could that be possible? "What about Grace?" he wondered aloud without intending to, not exactly knowing what he meant by the question.

The man's store-bought smile widened. "Charlie had a pretty young daughter rounding wit him. Peoples called her Cowboy's Girl. A real looker. Once she sat at the table, men like me had trouble concentratin' on the game, if you know what I means. She's the spittin' image of him."

"Is she?"

"Ain't it the trut'." He thrust his hand toward Ray, fingers splayed. "Name's Lewis Saint James."

"Ray Colton." Ray shook the man's hand, soft as a well-used chamois, then tossed a glance in Grace's direction as she lost another pot. "Tell me, Mr. Saint James, does this cowboy strategy work?"

"Depends on the player, son." Ray looked at him and Lewis Saint James winked. "Depends on the player."

~~~

Benny tried hard not to yawn but he couldn't help it. His scuba-diving watch said it was twelve o'clock. Johnny looked at his own giant watch and said, "We better head back before your dad thinks I've kidnapped you."

"'kay." Benny decided Johnny wasn't such a bad guy after all. "Thank you."

"You're welcome, kid."

They walked out of Circus Circus and Benny saw a tall, dark man standing in the middle of the sidewalk. He wore a wrinkled suit and had a sad color halo that made the air around him look bruised. His arms hung empty at his sides while he looked up and down the street like he lost something.

Benny forgot about being tired. He walked up to the man and stuck out his hand. "Hi. Benjaminraycolton."

The man frowned his lonely eyes at Benny and took his hand like he didn't know what else to do. "Edward Brown," he said.

Benny smiled. "I know. Come with me if you – "

26: All In

" – want to see Grace."

The man's big, warm hand tightened on Benny's. Not an angry tight. Desperate. "Do you know my Gracie?"

Benny nodded.

"Praise God. Where is she? Is she alright?"

"Yeah." Benny patted the back of his hand to make him feel better. "I'll show you."

"Hey, kid," Johnny leaned close and talked out the corner of his mouth, "how'd you know this guy was your friend's *esposo*?"

"Huh?"

"*Esposo*. It's Spanish for husband. See, I spent some time in Mex– " Johnny stopped and gave Grace's husband a quick look. "Never mind. That's another story. How'd you know?"

"His color."

Johnny's voice went low, like he had a secret to tell. "I got news for ya, kid. He ain't the only African American in Vegas."

Johnny might not be such a bad man, but he wasn't very smart, even if he did know Spanish. Benny didn't have time to explain it right now. "I know," he whispered back, then looked up at Grace's Eddy and asked, "Ready?"

"Yes, son."

~~~

The small of Grace's back ached and her bottom had gone numb. Nearly four hours at the poker table and her chip stack was still thirty grand short. She looked at her pocket sixes and wished they be aces or cowboys.

Dear Lord, thank you for the blessings you have already bestowed on me. If it be your will, please give me the cards I need to make this puny pair pay off Johnny's debt. I put my faith in your guiding hands. Amen.

Mr. Tony dealt trey, queen, six on the flop, giving Grace three of a kind. *Thank you, Jesus.* "Bet forty-five hundred," she said.

"Call." Mr. Tony matched her bet, burned the top card and dealt the turn.

Another six. *Praise the Lord and all his mercy.* Grace stared at the card a second or two before remembering herself. She tapped the table.

314

"Check."

Mr. Tony checked, dealt a jack on the river.

"Check," Grace said again, hoping the man across the table from her couldn't hear the mad pound of her pulse as she baited him.

"Bet fifteen thousand," Mr. Tony said.

Grace looked up at Moon and asked, "Would you happen to know the time?"

"It's midnight," he told her.

She sucked her teeth as though impatient, and pushed her entire chip stack to the center of the table. "All in."

Mr. Tony cocked his head. "Must be some date."

"History in the making," she replied vaguely. "B'sides, didn't you give Johnny 'til midnight?"

"I did." He studied her another moment, then shrugged as though it made no nevermind to him. "Since time is short," he pushed his chips to the middle of the table, "I call." He flipped over his pocket cards – two queens. Full house. He waited for her reaction, no doubt anticipating her disappointment.

Grace flipped over her two sixes. "Four of a kind."

~~~

"I'll be dogged," Lewis Saint James breathed.

"What is it?"

"Cowboy's Girl still gots it."

~~~

Grace heard the air pass between Mr. Tony's lips. "Congratulations," he said, and placed the remainder of the deck on the table, his movements slow and measured.

She gave him credit for his control, considering the trap he'd fallen into. Might be the money didn't mean that much to him. Or might be he really was as cold as Johnny said. Alligator blood. For Grace, the chips in the center of the table represented a whole lot more than their sum total. She culled her change from the pot, leaving $100,000 lie. "I believe that covers Johnny's debt?"

"It does."

Mr. Tony didn't seem inclined to shake hands, which suited Grace. But she meant it when she told him, "It's been a pleasure." She took Moon's offered hand and stood. The small of her back popped as she straightened. Before allowing Moon to escort her to the cashier's cage, she turned to Mr. Tony. "Mind if I ask a question?"

He looked up, gave a slight nod.

"Would you have had Johnny killed if he couldn't come up with your money by midnight?"

She felt Moon flinch. A cold smile crossed Mr. Tony's face. "'As he was valiant, I honored him; but, as he was ambitious...'"

I slew him. Brutus telling the crowd he killed Caesar so they could live as free men. Grace's papa told the story as a parable for civil liberty, but she doubted Mr. Tony had any notion of such things.

"It did not end well for Brutus," she remarked, and turned away from Mr. Tony's sterile laugh. She cashed in her poker chips, tucked the money in her purse and kissed Moon on the cheek. "Take care of yourself," she said.

"You do the same, Mrs. Grace."

She saw Ray waiting for her. His grin summed up her feelings fine. Next to him stood the gentleman with the unforgettable periwinkle eyes, doing his best to hold himself up straight, his grin outshining Ray's. He took his cowboy hat off at her approach, releasing an impressive mass of coily white hair.

"Lewis Saint James at your service," he said.

"That's not what they called you back in...Atlanta, wasn't it?"

"You've a good memory."

Lord have mercy, it felt nice to hear

somebody tell her that and mean it. She smiled. "What's not to remember, a handsome young man calling himself the Black Saint and flashin' his money around." Papa warned her to stay away from the sweet-talker turning ladies' heads. She didn't listen. Thankfully, Lewis Saint James had been more of a gentleman than her papa gave him credit for. "You remembered I like a lime wedge with my water," she said. "Thank you kindly."

"It'd be an honor if Cowboy's Girl 'd let me buy her a cup a coffee."

"I'm tempted," she told him truthful. Atlanta held some good memories. She hooked her arm in Ray's. "But I have a date with a casino."

"The Stardust." Saint James winked at her surprise. "Word got round 'bout what ol' Charlie and his girl did. Yep. Yep. Shame to lose the hist'ry."

"It ain't lost," Grace assured him. "Not long as people like you and me are still alive to remember it."

27: Adios

The sounds of a city revving toward its peak vibrated the night, the air dense with exhaust, fried food and acrid perfume. Headlights and neon stabbed Ray's dry pupils. He stopped at the corner of Roman's Bar and Burgers and looked down at Grace still holding his arm. Her expression outshined her loud pantsuit by a couple hundred watts.

"You keep grinnin' at me like that, Ray Colton," she said, her voice light, "I just might get the wrong impression."

Ray laughed. "It's been an evening to remember, hasn't it?"

"Lord have mercy, first time I've made that kind of money at a poker table." She released his arm and pulled a wad of bills from her purse. "I want you to have this."

"Naw, I can't – "

"Ain't no *can't* on this journey." She grabbed his hand and planted the money in his palm. "Haven't you figured that out yet?"

He couldn't argue with the truth. He fingered the bills in his hand. "There's five thousand dollars here."

She shrugged all matter-of-fact like. "It was a good night."

The money might help when it came time to pick up the Olds. "Thank you, Grace." He shoved the bills into his pocket and asked, "What are you going to do with your share?"

She grunted. "Buy sister Arleeta a new car."

Ray started to say something about being an honest thief, when he happened to glance over her shoulder at three figures coming up the walk, side by side. "Ben?"

Grace turned, leaned in a bit for a better look. "Who's that with him?" She took a hesitant step, shouted, "Eddy!" and broke into a run, leaving one of her sandals behind in her rush. The tall man at Benny's side opened his arms wide to envelop her.

Joy and loss hit Ray so hard he couldn't move without staggering under their weight.

~~~

Her man tasted of vanilla Moon Pies and

smelled of Brut aftershave laced with Bengay. Grace knew without asking, his arthritis troubled him. It always did when he sat too long. He must have driven straight through.

She ran her hand over his unshaved jaw. "Eddy, what are you doing here?"

He gave her an injured scowl. "You didn't think I'd sit at home and do nothing, did you?"

Of course he would come looking for her. It's what she would have done. "How did you find me?"

He tossed a glance over her shoulder. "Ask your young friend there."

Benny and Ray stood a short ways behind her, their arms around each other. Benny grinned and waved. Ray had a pained look on his face Grace identified with. Ed's arrival brought the end of their journey within touching distance. Her heart constricted. *I'm going to miss them two.*

Johnny interrupted the moment. "This is all very heartwarming, but what about me?" He spread his arms, palms up. "Am I a dead man standing here?"

"Your debt to Mr. Tony is paid," Grace said. She took $500 from her purse and handed it to him. "Here's your stake."

"I'll be damned. You really did it."

"Did what?" Ed asked. "Who's Mr. Tony? And why are you paying this man?"

Johnny pocketed his money and slapped his palms together. "That's my cue to vamoose."

"Stay outta trouble," Ray told him.

Johnny gave a mirthless hoot. "Yeah, right. You too." He tapped the brim of Benny's hat, knocking it down over the boy's eyes. "*Adios*, kid."

Benny pushed his hat back up and replied, "*Hasta la vista*."

Johnny winked. "See, you *do* know Spanish." With that, he turned and strutted away, his shiny pants catching flashes of neon and glitz.

"You think we'll ever see him again?" Grace asked.

Ray shrugged. "Hard to say."

"Will somebody please tell me what's going on?" Ed bellowed. Benny handed Grace her espadrille slide with its crimson flower. "And, woman, what are you wearing?"

~~~

Grace introduced her husband to Ray, then told him what she could as they made their way to an area with a view of the demolition. Too much had happened the past four days to sum up in a handful of minutes on a busy city street with dozens of others vying to see the fireworks. Ed already knew Ray and Benny were the ones God put in her path. She would save telling of Benny's special abilities to read and send for another day, though she thought her husband might have already witnessed a small taste. She told him about Johnny's bag of money, but being kidnapped and getting shot at would take a while to sort out and explain.

"The opportunity presented itself and I took it," she said when he asked about the poker game. "I had to prove to myself I could still do it."

"Did you get your answer? Or do you have more provin' to do?"

She glanced up at him walking beside her, saw the hard set to his jaw and the way he kept his eyes straight ahead. His way of steeling himself for a response he might not like. "I got my answer," she assured him. Papa would have been proud of the money stack she won this evening. She still had the moves, still had her wits, praise Jesus. Ray wasn't the only one who had lost faith in himself. Her panic attacks and fear had come from her own lack of faith. The poker game gave it back. But this weren't the life for her no more. Her nerves couldn't take it. "My poker days are behind me."

The steel lost its hold on her man and his

face relaxed. "That's too bad," he said after a moment. He quirked an eyebrow at her surprise. "It might be more interesting than bingo night."

"Eddy!"

He hugged her close. "You've changed, Gracie."

"Have I?"

"You're more sure of yourself. More like the woman I married."

She thought of his denial, how she'd scared him. How she'd scared herself. She steered him over to a broad pole, out of the way of the crowd, and stopped. Ray and Benny walked on ahead.

Grace turned Ed to look at her, saw the shine in his eyes and felt her own eyes prickle. "I'm here now," she told him, cupping his face in her hands. "Ain't nothin' going to change that."

"Praise the Lord," he breathed, and kissed her like he'd come home.

~~~

Fireworks shot from the top of the Stardust. "Cool!" Benny shouted.

People cheered as the pretty colors exploded high in the sky. The air filled with smoke and Benny sneezed. He heard somebody's car alarm honking.

After long minutes, the fireworks stopped and bright white lights went all the way around the building. Then big numbers on the front of the Stardust counted down.

"Ten! Nine! Eight!" Benny shouted with the crowd. Dad and Grace and Ed counted too. "Four! Three! Two! One!" More fireworks from the top of the building, then it went dark. Benny held his breath.

Boom! Boom! Boom! shook the ground like thunder. *Boom! Boom!* In slow motion, the bottom of the Stardust crumbled and the building leaned. The walls fell apart and a gray cloud rose into the air. Benny could see the ball of lights on the tower behind the Stardust because the Stardust was gone, nothing left but the gray cloud growing bigger and spreading across the parking lot. People got into their cars and started to leave.

"That's all?" Benny asked. When buildings got destroyed in the movies, they always burned up. Where was the fire?

"That's it," Dad said. "Just dust and rubble."

Benny sighed. Johnny was right. A lot of things only happened in the movies.

~~~

Once the last of the fireworks faded out,

they went back to the Harley so Grace could collect her belongings. "This is how you got here?" Ed asked.

"It's the Black Pearl," Benny informed him.

"I was the ballast," Grace said.

"Dear Lord."

Ray liked Ed. A patient man who clearly loved his wife, he tried hard to take it all in. One thing for certain, Grace wouldn't lack for stories to tell him on the drive back to Arkansas. Ray chuckled at the look her husband gave her when she handed him a pillowcase stuffed with her things. They'd had to leave their bulky suitcases at the hotel in Albuquerque

Seeing the two of them together brought to mind Virginia and how much he missed her. He knew in time the wound would scab over, lose its power to bring him to his knees. Like Rose said, he healed fast. But he knew there would be moments when the scab broke loose a little to remind him, too.

"I'm keeping my leathers," Grace said, "but you boys hang onto the helmet, case you find some other soul in need of rescuing." She lifted a saddlebag flap, almost absentminded like, then let it drop. "I s'pose that's everything."

Benny wrapped his arms around her middle

and cried softly into the bosom of her pantsuit jacket. She kissed his cheek and whispered something in his ear. Ray looked away and clenched his jaw against the growing pressure at the backs of his eyes.

Damn it. They all knew this time would come. But knowing didn't make it any easier.

"Ray honey."

He turned and Grace opened her arms to him. He stepped into them, rested his cheek on her hair, and quit trying to fight the tears. She patted his back as though soothing a child. "You're goin' to be alright," she told him. "I have faith in you."

So did he – now. And all because of her. When he was able to find his voice, goodbye felt too final. Instead, he said, "Any time you wanna hit the road again, you let us know."

Grace gave him a last squeeze, pulled back and asked, "Why do you think I'm hangin' onto my leathers?" Ray smiled with her. "If you gentlemen ever get to Little Rock, you're welcome to sit a spell." She drew a cocktail napkin from her purse and handed it to him. Ray saw the phone number written on it and lifted an eyebrow, intent on teasing her a mite, but she was already ahead of him and winked. "It be the right one."

Ed offered to buy them coffee but Ray didn't see any point in prolonging the inevitable. "Thanks, but I'd like to see the sunrise over the canyon. I reckon if my boy and I leave now, we can make it there in time."

28: The Eagle

"This better be good," Ray's brother growled low over the phone line.

Crap. I forgot what time it is. "Sorry, Frank. I didn't mean to wake you."

"Ray?"

"I can call back at a decent hour, if you want."

"Like I'd get any sleep wondering why my baby brother's calling me at...three thirty in the a.m.?"

"I'm in Las Vegas," Ray said by way of explanation. "You know...Sin City."

"Do tell. Is everything okay? What the hell you doing in Vegas?"

"It's a long story. Ben and I are headed for the Grand Canyon, then we'd like to drop in and see you and Barb, if that's alright."

"Who is it?" Ray heard Barb ask groggily in the background.

"It's Ray," Frank answered. "He and Benny wanna pay us a visit. Okay with you?"

"As long as I can finish sleeping first."

Frank chuckled. "When can we expect you?"

"Day after tomorrow. Maybe the next. There's a few things I want to show Ben between here and there." For the first time, he felt like he could slow down and enjoy the view. He still wanted to reach the Pacific Ocean, dig his toes in the sand, breathe deep of the salt air, but the guilt and anger that drove him to fly through eight states no longer dogged him. "You're still living in Sandy, right?"

"Yeah, but not long after we came home from Virginia's funeral, we moved across the highway. Bought the old Stinson place. Still got a lot of stuff in boxes, but we'll push things around and make room. Anyways, it's a square, two-story on Wolf Drive. Bright yellow. You can't miss it."

Ray stilled. His brother just described the crayon drawing Benny did a few days ago in an Oklahoma greasy spoon. Told Grace it was home. Ray hadn't bothered to correct him. He looked over at the bike parked at the curb.

Benny waved from the sidecar. Ray waved back. The kid was downright spooky sometimes.

"You still there?" Frank asked.

"Yeah," Ray said, returning his attention to the payphone. "We'll find it. Look for a pearl black Harley with a sidecar and two good-lookin' dudes in leathers."

Again his brother chuckled. "Can't wait to hear the story behind *that* one." Frank cleared his throat and lowered his voice. "You sure you guys are okay? I mean, it hasn't been long..."

"We're fine as frog's hair," Ray said. He looked back at his son. "This trip has been the best thing we could've done."

"Glad to hear it, brother. Glad to hear it."

~~~

The Grand Canyon looked just like in *Thelma & Louise*, only bigger. Lots bigger. Like a deep crack in the earth that Benny figured must go on for miles and miles.

Dad said, "You know we can't really fly over this thing, don't you?"

"Yeah." That only happened in the movies too.

The Colorado River weaved like a skinny green snake around stacks of red rocks. Orange and yellow streaks of sunlight made the canyon glow. Benny closed his eyes – *It's dangerous to stare at the sun*, Mama told him – and lifted his face to let the sun shine through his eyelids. It warmed the empty spot Grace's goodbye left in him. He missed her. Just like he missed Mama. Except something told him he would see Grace again. That made saying goodbye a little bit easier.

"Take care of your daddy," she whispered, and kissed his cheek.

A light breeze brushed his hair. It used to scare him to think about taking care of his daddy. He didn't think he was strong enough or smart enough. But now he knew better. He opened his eyes and looked over at the man standing straight and tall at his side. The blue sky behind his dad's head made him look invincible, another word Benny learned from Mama. She used to say the Terminator was invincible because nothing could stop him. But even the Terminator needed help sometimes. All good heroes did. Benny would be there when his daddy needed him.

An eagle flew over the canyon, right in front of them. "Look at that," Dad said, his voice low, like he didn't want the eagle to hear and be scared off.

They watched the bird soar and dip and

loop for a long time, like it was showing off. It made that laughing sound Benny remembered from before.

"You suppose it could be the same one?" Dad asked, saying out loud the question Benny had in his head.

Benny thought about it long and hard, and finally said, "It is."

The eagle laughed one more time, then tipped its wings and flew away.

"He's headed northwest," Dad said.

Benny nodded. "Oregon." It didn't sound right coming out of his mouth, but he knew his dad understood. And after a while he would learn to say it better.

"Reckon he knows we're going that way too?" Dad asked.

Benny smiled. He couldn't explain how he knew about Uncle Frank and Aunt Barbie's new yellow house. He just did. And he couldn't explain how he knew he and his dad would be staying there for a long time, but he did. It made him happy.

He took his dad's hand and said, "Home."

"Are you sure, son?"

"Yeah, Dad. Let's go."

Cindy Hiday

Acknowledgments

My heartfelt gratitude to the long list of family members, friends, and good folks in my writing workshop who read and re-read my story through its many transformations, gave me sincere feedback, and continually encouraged me to get the darn thing published.

Special thanks to Kris Ann for her insightful advice when Grace gave me grief. And, as always, a huge thank you to my trusted posse of editors: Julie, Kim, and Claudia. Their dedication and hard work keep my writing honest.

All my love to Jack, who not only created a fantastic cover, but lived with the early stages of this idea, endured some crazy detours, and somehow kept me grounded.

About the Author

Writing in the spirit of adventure and happy endings, Pacific Northwest author Cindy Hiday has won numerous honors, including first place in the Kay Snow Awards for Fiction from Willamette Writers. Her humorous literary novel, *Father, Son & Grace* (republished as *Destination Stardust*), is a five-star Readers' Favorite and local book club choice. When she isn't writing, Cindy enjoys growing her own produce, hiking old-growth forests in search of the next waterfall, and strolling long, sandy beaches.

cindyhiday.com